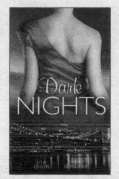
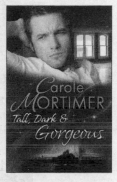
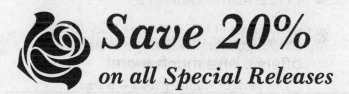

She's loved and lost — will she ever learn to open her heart again?

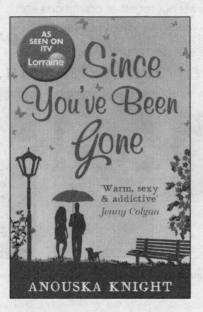

From the winner of ITV Lorraine's Racy Reads, Anouska Knight, comes a heart-warming tale of love, loss and confectionery.

'The perfect summer read — warm, sexy and addictive!'
—Jenny Colgan

For exclusive content visit:
www.millsandboon.co.uk/anouskaknight

0813/MB438

Wrap up warm this winter with Sarah Morgan...

Sleigh Bells in the Snow

Kayla Green loves business and hates Christmas.

So when Jackson O'Neil invites her to Snow Crystal Resort to discuss their business proposal... the last thing she's expecting is to stay for Christmas dinner. As the snowflakes continue to fall, will the woman who doesn't believe in the magic of Christmas finally fall under its spell...?

4th October

www.millsandboon.co.uk/sarahmorgan

1013/MB435

"You should go back. I'll take it from here."

"No way." Jo shook her head. "I didn't stick my neck out for you just to get a better view when they take you down."

"I'll land on my feet," Thomas insisted.

"This time I think you need someone to break the fall."

"If you stay, it could mean the end of your career. Or your life."

"I can take care of myself. You know you need someone watching your back."

He opened his mouth to protest. She pressed her fingers gently to his lips. "Don't say it. You have a partner this time. You'll just have to accept it."

His lips kissed her fingers. She yanked her hand back as if she'd been scalded. Before she could step back, he caught her and pulled her hard against his strong body.

BRIDAL
ARMOUR

BY
DEBRA WEBB

First published in Great Britain 2013
by Mills & Boon, an imprint of Harlequin (UK) Limited,
Eton House, 18-24 Paradise Road, Richmond, Surrey TW9 1SR

© Debra Webb 2013

ISBN: 978 0 263 90372 0
ebook ISBN: 978 1 472 00742 1

46-0913

Harlequin (UK) policy is to use papers that are natural, renewable and recyclable products and made from wood grown in sustainable forests. The logging and manufacturing processes conform to the legal environmental regulations of the country of origin.

Printed and bound in Spain
by Blackprint CPI, Barcelona

Debra Webb wrote her first story at age nine and her first romance at thirteen. It wasn't until she spent three years working for the military behind the Iron Curtain and within the confining political walls of Berlin, Germany, that she realized her true calling. A five-year stint with NASA on the space-shuttle program reinforced her love of the endless possibilities within her grasp as a storyteller. A collision course between suspense and romance was set. Debra has been writing romance, suspense and action-packed romance thrillers since. Visit her at www.debrawebb.com or write to her at PO Box 4889, Huntsville, AL 35815, USA.

Chapter One

"I don't know how the pilot managed, but we landed safely." Thomas Casey relaxed his grip on his cell phone and drew in his first deep breath since the pilot had announced a sudden winter storm had hit Denver only minutes before their scheduled landing. The storm had descended rapidly and with the same ferocity as the Bronco Blizzard from another mid-October day a few decades ago.

According to the weather update Thomas had caught on a local newscast since his flight arrived, the forecast called for at least a foot of snow in the coming twenty-four hours. The temperature had dropped dramatically in the past hour, icing the streets of the city and threatening to shut down every form of transportation.

"Any chance you're getting out of there this afternoon?" Lucas Camp, Thomas's longtime friend and colleague, asked, hope in his tone.

As soon as he'd gotten off that damned plane, Thomas had put through a call to Lucas. His old friend and his wife, Victoria Colby-Camp, were already ensconced in the small village resort where the wedding would take place.

Despite being a twenty-year veteran of black ops,

Thomas felt his knees weaken just a little. He'd never been married nor had children of his own. Casey Manning, his niece, was like a daughter to him. When she'd asked him to give her away at her wedding, he'd choked up so damned bad he could scarcely cough out an answer. Casey was his sister, Cecelia's, only child. Cecelia's husband had passed away suddenly just a year ago. Standing in was the least Thomas could do.

If he could get out of this damned airport.

"It'll take a hell of a lot more than a little snow to keep me away from that wedding," Thomas promised. "You tell my niece I'll be there."

The village was only two hours from Denver, half the distance from here to Aspen. He'd crawled across deserts in the Middle East and scaled mountains in the dead of winter in Eastern Europe. How hard could it be to manage a hundred or so snow-covered miles in Colorado?

"The rehearsal dinner isn't until tomorrow night," Lucas reminded him. "Tonight's reception is just a casual affair. Stay in the city until morning if the roads are too hazardous for safe travel."

Thomas grinned. "I think you're getting soft, Lucas." The next thing he'd be telling Thomas was to be sure to wear his seat belt—which he did anyway. "Ordinarily you'd be suggesting I find myself a pair of cross-country skis and hoof it on over to your location."

A belly laugh boomed across the connection. "I can see you've never been a member of a wedding party, old friend. Once wedding plans are in place, God help the unfortunate soul who throws a wrench in the works. The sweetest young woman will become bridezilla in a heartbeat. I'm not worried about you, Thomas. It's those of us already here with the bride-to-be who have to worry."

"I'll be there, Lucas." Thomas ended the call and tucked

his cell into his pocket. He picked up his carry-on and followed the signs to the lower level and ground transportation.

JOHARA DEROSSI'S HEART was still lodged in her throat. The way the storm had dropped on the city, she'd been convinced Thomas Casey's plane would ice up and tumble to the runway like a radio-controlled toy with no battery life. While that might have put a convenient end to her task here, it wasn't at all how Thomas Casey should leave this world.

The enigmatic director of Mission Recovery owed his country an explanation—her, too, if she was being honest. But her questions were not the priority.

Having disguised herself as one of the many flight attendants from a nearby airline milling about deciding how and where to wait out the storm, she'd cloned his cell phone. Now, listening in on her target's phone call, she silently thanked Lucas Camp for helping her cause. If the wedding party wasn't expecting him to arrive until tomorrow, she had a head start.

As Thomas left the gate area for the lower levels, she trailed at a respectable distance, but kept him in sight. He couldn't be crazy enough to try to pick up his rental car in this weather. She had to presume he'd call a hotel for availability and then pick up a ride on a courtesy shuttle. It really didn't matter. He wasn't going to make it that far anyway.

What did matter was that her window of opportunity was closing fast, the already tight schedule accelerated by the storm. Good thing she thrived on pressure or she'd need serious medication about now.

As a member of the Initiative committee, the small group charged with the oversight of ultra-covert teams like Casey's Mission Recovery Specialists, her life was rarely dull.

When his name had crossed her desk, along with the report listing the privileged information that had roused the suspicions against him, she had immediate and mixed reactions.

She didn't want to believe it. Men weren't built any more dedicated or patriotic than Thomas Casey. The idea that he may be guilty of treason—or worse—made her stomach churn. As an investigator, she knew better than to prejudge an operative or a situation, but Thomas was different. She didn't want to go digging into his past, but more important, she didn't want anyone else digging into it.

On some level she recognized just how screwed up that was.

Be that as it may, having served with him on a mission near the time period in question, she was eminently qualified. With that in mind, she'd checked his schedule and counted it good fortune that she would be able to deal with this away from the prying eyes in Washington, D.C.

She walked by him as Thomas paused near the rental car lines and pulled out his phone. Listening in again, she was pleased by his predictable behavior as he made his first call to a nearby hotel. Smart man, she thought, as he booked the room without blinking at the storm-inflated price. The hotel clerk promised the next shuttle would be at the appropriately marked stand within ten minutes.

Adjusting her timetable for the shuttle and the road conditions, Jo started for the parking garage. It took all her control not to skid to a stop when she spotted another familiar face among so many strangers.

Specialist Jason Grant, one of Thomas Casey's rising stars, was coming down the escalator. Though his eyes were shadowed by dark glasses, she knew his gaze was sweeping the crowd.

Damn it. She'd checked the itineraries for all of Thomas's team over the next week. Grant wasn't slated to attend the wedding. According to her information, he should have been working recon on a new case in Vegas. With one conversation, he could ruin her plans for a clean capture. She had only seconds to head him off.

Well, that's what plan B was for, she mused. Jo popped open one more button on her blouse and rushed back toward Thomas. "Excuse me, sir? Seat A2, right?"

His brow puckered and she knew he was trying to place her from the airplane. "I worked coach," she explained. "But I spotted this in your seat on my way out."

She flashed an overly bright smile and handed him a passport. "That's you, right?"

He opened it and, startled, gazed up at her. "Who are you?"

"You know me," she murmured, leaning closer. "Thomas."

His eyes went wide as he recognized her voice under the disguise.

"I need you." The words were out, full of more truth than she cared to admit regarding their past, present and quite possibly their immediate future.

He nodded once, all business, and fell in beside her as she headed toward an employee access. She refused to look back, though she could feel Grant closing in as the door locked behind them.

"This way."

"Tell me what's going on, Jo."

She ignored the ripple of awareness that followed his using her given name. It wasn't the reaction she'd expected. Thomas always treated everyone with efficient professionalism. Except for that one notable, extremely personal, incident years ago.

"I'll tell you everything just as soon as we're out of here." She checked her watch. They had less than five minutes before the cabbie she'd paid to wait left in search of another fare. In this weather they'd never find another taxi. "Keep up. We have to get out of the area before the roads are closed." She'd taken precautions, given herself options, but no one could prepare for a freak blizzard.

"Are you in trouble?"

"Yes." On one too many levels, she realized. But it was too late to back out now. If she didn't follow through, someone more objective would take over the investigation. Based on what she'd seen, she didn't think that was a good idea.

Moving forward, she hoped some deep-seated instinct kicked in, making him curious enough to cooperate with her. Grant wasn't just one of his Specialists, he was the best of the current crop. He'd been tagged to replace Deputy Director Holt, the man who held the position in which Lucas Camp had once served, when the deputy eventually moved up to replace Thomas.

The Initiative committee had approved the plan. Right now, she wondered what the hell they'd been thinking.

"Jo, wait."

Would the day ever come when his voice didn't create that shiver of anticipation? "No time."

"I need an explanation."

"And I'll give you one when we're away from the airport."

"Jo." He caught her arm, forced her to stop and really look at him.

Airport employees passed by, moving to and from their respective duties with various degrees of interest in their obviously strained interaction. She made mental notes, knew he was doing the same. Always an eye out for the next threat.

"A particular German mission file crossed my desk last week."

"I see."

She fingered the disk in her pocket. Loaded with enough sedative to guarantee his cooperation, she hesitated to use it. And she knew without reservation that she would get only one chance. "This was the only time we could talk safely." Or so she'd thought.

"I've booked a hotel room," he said. "We can talk there."

"Fine." Better if he believed she'd willingly compromise. "I have a cab waiting."

At last he fell into step beside her once more, giving her hope this would go well. It almost felt like old times. *Almost*.

Back then she thought they'd been on the same page, working together toward a common goal. After five years apart on diverging career paths, after reading through so many reports of success from his Specialists who routinely went above and beyond mission parameters, she wasn't sure they could ever be on the same page again.

She might be sure he wasn't a traitor, she just wasn't so sure anymore that she was in the same league as the man behind the stoic, black ops armor.

Chapter Two

Mission Recovery Specialist Jason Grant had successfully shadowed Agent DeRossi to Denver, Colorado. On her tail for several days, he knew the hotel she'd been staying in wasn't within government per diem limits and, thanks to the GPS tag he'd put on her rental, he'd learned she liked to shop in ritzy boutiques.

For as long as he'd been tracking her, he hadn't recognized any of her contacts. If Deputy Director Holt hadn't sent him out here personally, he might think this was a wild goose chase. As it was, he was starting to question the rumor claiming she was here on a Mission Recovery witch hunt. Didn't look that way to him.

Her return to the airport in a flight attendant uniform piqued his curiosity. He hoped whoever she was here to meet appreciated her effort. She looked pretty damned hot.

He'd followed her through the terminal, but if she'd made contact with anyone, it had been too subtle for him to catch. As a well-trained and experienced member of Mission Recovery, getting something by him was highly unlikely and the thought that she'd managed it made him nervous. And definitely ticked him off.

Beyond the windows of the airport, the storm rolled down from the mountains like an avalanche, blanketing the city with snow and ice. He didn't care for the idea of being stuck in an airport with thousands of stranded travelers, so it was a relief when DeRossi finally started to move.

Until he lost her.

Her curly blond wig was gone. The bright red blazer of the airline she'd falsely represented was absent from the crowd of travelers milling about. He cursed his arrogance. His boss had warned him she was top of the game, but Jason hadn't been concerned. The woman had been riding a desk for more than three years. However sharp she had once been, she couldn't be on the top of her game these days.

His gaze continued to roam the crowd. She hadn't been that far ahead of him. He tucked himself into a place at the end of the escalators where he could keep an eye on the restrooms as well as the main path to baggage claim.

He gave it three long minutes before he admitted the truth. She'd gotten away. Because she'd spotted him or because she'd completed whatever she'd been sent to do here?

He dialed Deputy Director Holt but the call went straight to voice mail. Probably for the best. Reporting a screw-up like losing the target was way, way low on the list of his favorite activities.

Other than telling him to watch her and report her activities, no one had really briefed him on the real reason why DeRossi was in Colorado at the same time as Director Casey. Having her in the airport at the time of his arrival had to be more than coincidence, but so far as he'd been able to observe she hadn't made contact.

He'd never met a field agent who liked oversight divisions—whether it was the Internal Affairs divisions of police departments or the covert equivalent of the Initiative committee.

An airport security cart whizzed by and Jason decided it was time to get creative. If he could get into the security office, maybe he'd get lucky and spot her on one of the many video feeds they monitored.

He considered fabricating an elaborate story and settled on a lower-risk version of the truth. Following the cart to the nearest security team office, he walked in, credentials ready.

"Can I help you?"

Jason flipped open the wallet with a badge and ID card as he surveyed the entire space. The security office setup was familiar. One uniformed person at the desk, a couple of others in offices that overlooked the small reception area. He glanced at the one closed door and assumed that was where all the real information was hidden.

"Good afternoon." He smiled, throwing in a little charm since the uniform was female. "I'm Agent Grant. I was tailing a suspect and she managed to ditch me at baggage claim," he said with just the right blend of irritation and embarrassment. It was a skill he'd picked up during his time in law enforcement.

"I need a look at your cameras, see if I can spot her. Consider it a professional courtesy," he added. "I really don't want to have to hear about this mistake for the rest of my life, if I can avoid it."

She smiled just a little and made a call to her immediate superior. Feeling the eyes on him, he let his shoulders slump as he tucked his badge away, playing the part of the guy who was having a bad day.

It worked. She hung up the phone and walked him over to the closed door.

Two men in airport security uniforms watched the cycling views of the area from the escalators to the exit doors on the wide bank of monitors. Reading the labels under each, he soon had a feel for each area covered by the closed-circuit cameras.

Public areas, employee-only access and the walkways and streets just outside the terminal. *Where was she?* She wasn't loitering in baggage claim. Not in the rental car line either.

"Who are you looking for?"

"Flight attendant. Female. Blonde. In a red blazer." And with less than a minute a good operative could have changed any one of those distinguishing features. He'd given her three minutes plus the time it had taken him to get in here.

DeRossi was an oversight agent. Hadn't pushed anything more dangerous than paper in a couple of years. He wanted to bang his head against the wall for underestimating her. No one working any aspect of covert ops got hired or moved up the food chain by accident.

Still. She'd shown no sign of spotting him tailing her and it wasn't entirely unreasonable to believe her field skills would be rusty.

"Hot?" one of the guards asked.

"Aren't they all?" Grant mused.

"Sure," the guard admitted with a smirk. "But a few stand out. Let me cue this for you."

Jason waited the few seconds, let the guard zoom in. "Yeah, that's her," he said, stopping just shy of a fist pump. DeRossi strolled down an employee access hall with a businessman at her side. There was a brief conversation, then they moved again, out of the camera's view. "Where did she go?"

"Got her," the other guard said. "She went into a cab with the dude."

Jason nearly choked when he recognized the man in the picture. Director Casey was no one's "dude." It wasn't his job to know what DeRossi wanted with the head of his division, but of all the possibilities that popped into his head, none of them were good. The director was here for a family event and with no ties to the bride or groom, DeRossi wasn't on the guest list.

Hell. Had he just allowed the director to be kidnapped?

Feeling more than a little grim, Jason watched the cab pull away from the curb. Without being asked, the pair of guards brought up visuals from the other cameras stationed around the airport until the cab went completely out of their range.

"The cab is in the lane for the long-term parking lots."

That didn't make sense to him. The car DeRossi drove to the airport was parked in the short-term garage. He'd parked on the other end of the same level.

"Don't airline employees have their own lot?"

"Sure," the first guard said. "If they're based here, most of the crews take a shuttle in from home. But if she's with him…" The guard let that thought trail off, but they all knew what he was implying. A sexual rendezvous wasn't something Jason wanted to think about either.

"Can you cue up a view of those lots?"

The second guard shook his head. "Closed circuit on a different system through another security contract. Sorry."

"No problem." He had a general direction at any rate and the storm would slow her down. He hoped. A situation like this was all about the legwork and though she had a head start, he wasn't out of the game.

His phone rang and the screen showed Deputy Director Holt's somber face. Jason answered, braced to admit his momentary setback.

"I just received a new alert of a potential problem child in your area. I'm sending you the picture."

Problem child in this context could mean anything from an informant to an assassin. "Am I being reassigned?" He wanted to ask more questions, but wouldn't risk it in front of the guards.

"No. Watch for the paths to cross."

"If they do?"

"Document, but do not intervene."

Whoa. That set off all of his internal alarms. "Yes, sir."

"Any news for me?"

He thought of DeRossi and Casey in the cab and out of his reach. "Not at this time."

"You lost her," Holt said with an irritable sigh.

"Not exactly." It wasn't a lie. He still had a general direction. "This freak storm is slowing everything down."

"I need to know what she's after. ASAP."

"Yes, sir," Jason replied. "I'm on it."

Ending the call, he turned the phone back and forth in his hands, waiting for the picture to come through. When it did he gave a low whistle. A woman with fiery red hair and a grin as satisfied as a cat with a mouthful of canary filled his screen. He vaguely wondered what she'd been doing when the photographer had captured the candid shot. He had the disquieting sense that he'd seen her before. Though he couldn't place her immediately, he knew it would come to him.

Shaking off the errant thought, he considered how to fulfill his orders. Regrettably, he didn't have much choice but to go back to square one: DeRossi's hotel room. He'd searched yesterday and turned up nothing useful. Not even that uniform.

Damn. He'd been played by an expert whose day job of riding a desk was apparently no indication of what she was capable of. The fact that she and his boss were headed by cab to long-term parking when Jason had followed her to the short-term garage initially meant she had a backup vehicle. The logical conclusion was she had a secondary hotel room, too.

Damn.

"Can you access the cameras from the gate areas?" Jason provided the terminal number where he'd found DeRossi this morning. He hoped going back to where she'd been would give him a clue about where she was headed with the director.

Reviewing the video footage from the cameras near the gates did nothing but affirm he hadn't missed a drop or exchange. She might have done a little shopping in recent days, but everything now pointed to her coming here solely to grab Director Casey.

Thanking the security team, he exited the office and headed for the parking garage. Holt expected a new player to intersect with either DeRossi, Casey or both of them. He had to pick up the trail.

Casey had hired Jason into Mission Recovery. Jason wasn't sure he could sit back and do nothing but document any danger aimed at the director. As a Specialist, his job was to salvage missions that had gone beyond the hope of regular recovery. Holt knew that, knew the philosophy of the Specialists. Did the deputy director really expect Jason to go against the order to stay out of whatever was going on here? Was he relying on the Specialist philosophy of running toward danger rather than away from it?

Jason struggled to make sense of the limited data he had, to organize that data into the context of the orders Holt had handed down.

The Initiative jumped on internal investigations like kids jumped on candy after the piñata breaks. DeRossi had carte blanche to do anything in the name of her official inquiry. And apparently not even Holt knew precisely what she was after. Did that include giving someone a chance to take out the director? Jason's gut clinched.

None of it lined up.

What could be so bad that execution was the best answer?

The better question was did anyone, including the deputy director, really believe Jason would stand back and let that happen?

Frustrated, he turned up the collar on his suit coat, not nearly enough protection against the blizzard. Staring out into the storm, he guessed there were two inches of snow on the ground already and about ten more on the way. He had to pick a direction and get moving.

Jason remembered Director Casey's answer when he asked why he'd been selected to join the Specialists. "You have the best instincts I've seen in a long time."

His instincts were on high alert but he just had to figure out where to aim them.

Casey was here for a wedding. Jason turned in the general direction of the mountain resort hosting the event. Somewhere behind the blizzard was a chalet with a fatherless bride counting on her uncle to walk her down the aisle in just over forty-eight hours. Jason felt his temper rising at the idea that he was supposed to observe and document if the director was threatened.

But anger would only blur the instincts.

Evidence to the contrary, in this weather, he couldn't see DeRossi going anywhere other than her hotel room to wait out the storm, no matter what her primary plans had been. If DeRossi was out to make a statement, the wedding party was full of covert operatives from Specialists to Colby Agency investigators with plenty of history and exemplary service records. There could be any number of reasons for her to intercept Casey here and now.

A cold wind blew through the parking garage and he took it in, clearing his head. His decision made, he turned back to his car, just as a flash of orange caught his peripheral vision. He spun around, watching an oily black cloud beat back the storm in one small spot among the endless fields of parked cars.

Car bomb.

Something entirely too much like fear detonated in his gut.

Busy airport or not, he just couldn't believe the explosion was a coincidence. Jason raced to see if losing De-Rossi had meant the death of his director.

Chapter Three

Thomas hadn't stayed alive as the head of Mission Recovery by relying on luck or anyone's mercy. He tried to tell himself he was following this woman out of professional courtesy, but it didn't work. DeRossi was a weakness. One he'd purposely culled from his life years ago. He'd never had any real objectivity where this woman was concerned.

They'd parted as friends—or so he'd thought—until she'd landed on the Initiative committee.

Knowing she could look over his shoulder, question any or all of his decisions had only affirmed his choice to avoid a personal relationship—with her or anyone else. In this line of work you could have the job or the life, but not both.

A tiny voice in his head suggested his niece and her soon-to-be husband disproved his theory. What might work for her, however, would never work for him. He was too set in his ways and there was an inherent distance he didn't think he could bridge.

He scowled, thinking back to those days working with Jo. They'd been good as partners and he'd assumed their chemistry had been more about the rush of fieldwork than any real connection. Except he'd never quite gotten her out of his system.

"Tonight is all you get. I have to be at the Glenstone Lodge by tomorrow."

She nodded once.

"For Casey's wedding."

She nodded again.

"She asked me to give her away."

Jo slanted him a look with those midnight eyes, then, without comment, pushed open the exit door.

Cold air, swirling with heavy, wet snowflakes, battered them. Visibility was bad even though they were protected by the terminal building. He glanced up. The mountain peaks weren't even a shadow on the horizon. The roads to Glenstone were probably already closed. "Lord, what a storm."

More silence from Jo as she stepped into the miserable weather.

He reached to button his coat, belatedly realizing she didn't have anything warmer than the flight attendant's uniform blazer.

"Take this." He draped his overcoat across her shoulders. She graced him with a small, tight smile and rushed toward a waiting taxi. He didn't know how she managed it on those needles she called heels.

"I was about to give up on you, lady," the driver said as they slid into the welcome warmth of his cab.

"What does he mean by that?" Warnings clanged in Thomas's head even as he closed the door. He could overpower her, but he was too curious about what she was really after.

She shot him a look that confirmed he already knew the answer. He gave her points for remembering her field training and planning more than one exit.

Thomas gave the name of the hotel and the driver pulled away from the curb. The typical airport traffic was lighter on the employee access route, but the cab fishtailed a bit in the worsening conditions. He hoped the driver knew which way was which, because Thomas had no idea. It wasn't quite a whiteout, but the wind had picked up and was blowing snow sideways across the car.

"Hard to believe this is October," Jo said with a subtle nod toward the driver.

"Looks more like January," Thomas agreed.

He had questions for her, all of which had to wait until they were alone. He heard an alert on his phone and pulled it from his pocket.

He frowned, recognizing Deputy Director Holt's personal number on the missed call list. Thomas had left clear instructions for the current cases. He scrolled down to check messages, but between the heaters on high and the interrupted signal he couldn't make out anything but "committee." Sitting next to Jo, he assumed Holt was trying to give him a heads up about her.

"Problem?" Her smile was tight and her hands were in her pockets again.

Thomas shook his head. "Nothing Holt can't handle."

That answer only seemed to increase her anxiety as her lips thinned and she crossed her arms. When the cabbie turned toward long-term parking rather than the outlying circle of airport hotels, Thomas couldn't ignore his instincts any longer.

Slowly, his gaze locked with hers, he tucked the phone back in his pocket. Slower still, he placed his hands, fingers spread wide, on his thighs.

When she didn't move, he arched a brow.

Finally, she followed suit, showing him her hands were empty before folding them in her lap. "Truce?"

"Too soon to tell," he replied with brutal honesty.

"I know this is unexpected," she said, her voice pitched too low for the cab driver to overhear. "Work with me. Please."

He thought of the wedding plans, of his beautiful niece turning into a lace-covered bridezilla monster and decided both he and Lucas had faced tougher challenges. The rehearsal and dinner was hardly optional, but given his current predicament—unarmed in a blizzard with an obviously determined and still-talented agent who had clearly made an effort to get his attention…

"You have twenty-four hours."

She nodded, her tension easing fractionally.

"I will *not* miss her wedding."

"Agreed."

He thought it was an odd response, but the cab pulled to a stop behind a beige compact SUV and their conversation halted.

She paid the driver while he retrieved their bags from the trunk. When the parking lights flashed indicating she'd unlocked the vehicle, he opened the back hatch and put their luggage inside. The engine rumbled to life, startling him, and he looked over his shoulder to confirm she was controlling the car.

"Remote start," she said hurrying over.

He suddenly caught a whiff of an unmistakable odor of a lighted fuse, a precise scent he'd hoped never to come across again.

"Should have remembered it soon—"

"Jo, run!" But she kept moving closer to the car.

Throwing himself at her, he took them both to the icy pavement. He rolled them into the driving lane, his body the only shelter he could offer.

In his mind, it was Germany all over again, right down to the snowy conditions.

The blast of heat washed over them, obliterating the car and, for a moment, the blizzard conditions. The pavement shook with the force of the car dropping back down to earth and the detached, analytic part of his brain wondered just how high it had blown.

He risked a glance toward the ball of fire. The luggage had been vaporized in the explosion. His clothes, his irreplaceable surprise for Casey and whatever Jo had packed for her little venture were long gone. Reactions and assessment had to wait for later. Right now, they needed to move. Easing his grip on Jo, he looked into her midnight eyes, and weighed the sincerity of the shock and terror he saw there.

He knew she could be a consummate actress; it went along with their line of work. Various scenarios cycled through his mind, all of them bleak. Was she the perp or the victim? Had this been an attempt on her life or his? Both? Maybe she'd changed her mind about killing him or maybe the timing came down to a faulty fuse or signal on the bomb?

He wanted answers, but survival was first and foremost. Going separate ways seemed like the most prudent solution in light of the current circumstances. But the phrase "keep your friends close and your enemies closer" kept nudging him. Was Jo a friend or enemy?

Uncertain, he made his decision based on their relationship prior to her role with the Initiative committee.

"Are you hurt?"

"No." Snowflakes caught in her long eyelashes. "You?"

He gave a snort, but before he could answer, her eyes went wide and she flipped him onto his back. "Your jacket was on fire," she explained.

Well, her quick thinking and the deep slush seeping through the fabric had put it out now. He made a mental note that her reflexes and physical ability seemed to be in perfect order. It wasn't all that comforting considering his seemed to be a bit sluggish.

"Thanks." He pulled his cell phone from his pocket, removed the battery and tossed both pieces into the fiery wreckage. "Give me yours."

She scowled, but did the same with her own cell phone.

"Now let's move. Stay low."

"I know the protocol," she snapped, anger clear in her eyes, intensifying the flags of color high in her cheeks.

The attitude was a good sign. Maybe. He just didn't have enough facts to sort out the situation. "Prove it."

"That car was rented in your name. I changed your reservation and picked it up for you days ago," she answered before he could ask the obvious question. She held up a key fob with the logo of a different make. "My car is two rows that way."

He nodded and motioned for her to lead. Again.

They moved quickly through the lot, but he knew anyone could be watching, waiting for the right opportunity to pick them both off.

How had the bomb been triggered? And who wanted him dead? There were a number of possible answers to both questions. He mentally narrowed the list to people who wanted to eliminate them both, but that left him plenty of names to consider. And only sprouted more questions as he wondered who knew they were both in the area.

When they reached her car, he noted the license plate and watched her use a compact from her purse to check the undercarriage for problems.

She nodded, convinced it was safe, and they climbed inside. He suspected she was holding her breath the same as he was as she turned the key in the ignition. When the engine came to life and they were still intact, he buckled his seat belt. The action had him thinking of Lucas, and wondering how best to alert his friend to the developing situation.

"What's your plan?" He cranked up the heater and defrosters while she backed out of the parking space.

"Get out of Denver with all haste."

He had the wet, singed clothes on his back, his wallet and quickly dwindling options. "I hope you have something a little more detailed in mind." Her lips were pursed and quirked to the side, a sure sign she was thinking. "Go on, spill it." Maybe he'd get lucky and she'd give him something he could work with. "You used to like having a sounding board."

She peered up at the gray sky and he thought this time she might keep her theories to herself. "I'm wondering how you bribe Mother Nature?"

"Pardon me?"

"The storm almost took down your plane."

"You saw the landing?"

She nodded. "The storm certainly gives an assassin the advantage since you'd be trapped here overnight."

"Disadvantage," he argued. "The storm traps the assassin, too."

She slid a look his way as she merged onto the Interstate. "I'm not the assassin."

He wanted to believe her. "Says the woman who dropped me off at a car rigged to explode."

"Relax. I would have been beside you if I hadn't been picking my way through the snow. It took me back to that night in Germany."

Recalling the way she'd fiddled with the contents of her pockets, he reached across the seat and searched her.

Conditions were so bad, she had to keep both hands on the wheel and couldn't counter his search, but she called him all kinds of names in the interim. He didn't find a remote for the destroyed car, but his fingers closed on a small, flat disk sealed in a thick plastic envelope the size of a quarter.

"Not the assassin?" He held it up then snatched it back when she made a grab. The car swerved and a loud rumble growled around them as the tires rolled over the grooved pavement meant to alert a drifting driver.

"*Not* the assassin," she insisted. "That is just a light sedative. I brought it along in case you weren't inclined to cooperate."

"Any other surprises planted on you?"

"Wouldn't you like to know?"

Yes, he would. Her sly smile wasn't encouraging his trust but it was stirring other feelings he had no business allowing just now.

"Thomas, I know it looks bad," she said, her tone quiet and serious. "But I am on your side."

"I can't even call in my people to assess the device," he grumbled.

"But—"

"What?"

"Nothing."

"Everyone I trust is at the top of a mountain." Without a phone, he couldn't immediately reach the offices in D.C. He leaned forward, trying to see anything through the storm. "A mountain I can't even see. We should stop and buy a phone," he added, spotting a bright neon sign for a superstore.

"Not just yet."

He swiveled in his seat. "We've got a tail?"

"No. But I'd rather put the airport farther behind us before either one of us swipes a credit card."

Thomas took it as a bad sign that he hadn't been thinking about that. Sure, he'd flown out here for a wedding and left business to his deputy director, Emmett Holt, but that didn't give him the luxury of being rattled by events.

"What the hell does the Initiative committee want with me that couldn't wait until Monday?"

"I can't tell you right this minute."

"Jo—" He couldn't finish the threat. She jerked the wheel right and nearly lost control of the car in an effort to get to the exit ramp.

"Tail?"

"Yes." She laid on the horn and blew through the light at the end of the ramp. "There's a gun taped under your seat."

She pulled a hard left at the next corner and, with him reaching for the gun, his head rapped the door. On a curse, he powered down the window. Maybe the blast of cold air would have the added benefit of an ice pack.

"Stay in the left lane," he ordered. Thankfully traffic was sparse with the storm keeping most sane people safe inside. "Let him get closer."

"Are you nuts?"

"I'm open to better ideas." When she slowed down, he assumed she didn't have another suggestion.

The car pulled up beside them. The heavily tinted glass made it impossible to identify the driver, but the dark, menacing barrel of the handgun poking out of the back window made the intent clear enough.

He was ready to shoot out the front tire when Jo muscled the SUV into a spin. Like a boxer going for the knock-out punch, she used her bigger vehicle against the smaller sedan, connecting and driving the vehicle into a traffic light post. The impact crumpled the hood of the sedan and left them disabled in the roadway.

She shifted into Reverse and for a split second he thought she intended to ram the other car again, but she turned the steering wheel and sped away.

In the side mirror he caught the flash of a gun muzzle and braced for impact, but the bullets went high and wide.

They were alone as she turned the corner and revved the engine to make the next light. Finally they were back on the Interstate and going westbound this time. They were headed into the storm, but maybe conditions would improve as they worked their way up the mountain while the storm rolled east and out over Denver.

Chapter Four

5:55 p.m.

Jason wasn't the first on the scene of the explosion, but he was the first who had any idea what he was looking at. He flashed his badge and picked up what clues were available to the trained observer. The few people in the area of the explosion didn't have much useful information. One man noticed a cab leaving the row at about the same time. He thought the backseat had been empty.

No one saw a man or woman leaving the scene, but Jason knew Director Casey wouldn't have advertised his escape. And the snowfall, while melted away by the heat of the explosion, was coming down fast enough to blur any footprints leading away from the area.

Jason searched anyway. He looked at several empty spaces, making notes of the locations in case he could get a look at the video surveillance.

Studying the lot, he turned a full circle. Whoever had parked the car had done so with careful thought to the cameras and shuttle stops. That smacked of someone organized like DeRossi.

He found the license plate a couple rows away where it was still warm enough to melt the snow trying to cover it. He didn't touch it, just placed a call to the Mission Recovery analyst on duty and asked her to run the information. Within moments he learned the car was registered to a rental car agency and had been rented in Director Casey's name. Two days ago.

DeRossi.

Director Casey might have made the reservation, but no way he'd picked it up. Two days ago, the director had been in D.C. Unsure how Agent DeRossi had managed this with him on her tail, he made a note to ask her as soon as he had her cornered. And he would get her cornered.

Holt was going to hang him out to dry when word got back that Jason had misplaced the director. He was alive, that much was clear, but for how long? Out of options and with the wail of more sirens closing in, Jason stalked back to his car.

He opened the door and was about to slide behind the wheel when another flash of color caught his eye. Distinctive red hair was swept back into a high bun. She might have been another traveler distracted by the commotion, but something in the way she was looking over the scene put his instincts on alert.

When she looked his way, he recognized her as the woman Holt asked him to watch out for. Even without the heads up, he would have known she was involved. It was the sly, satisfied tilt of her mouth that didn't match the shock of the innocent bystanders. Was she the bomb builder? The trigger man—woman? He resisted the urge to walk over and confront her directly.

Instead, he went back and exchanged information with the officers on scene, giving her a chance to make an exit so he could follow her. It was a long shot, but if she didn't lead him to DeRossi, maybe she'd lead him to the people behind the plan to blow up Director Casey's car.

Without a cap or scarf, she obviously wasn't trying to

blend in. Hair like hers would be memorable to the dullest of eyewitnesses. He was grateful for her confidence, as that striking hair made it easy to keep her in his periphery with the rest of the world muted by blowing snow. Did she know, as he did, that Casey and DeRossi had escaped the trap?

When he saw her striding away, he quickly returned to his car, prepared to follow her until he had some answers. Choosing the lane closest to the building, he paid the parking fee and pulled through the gate, then stopped just behind the small building to wait.

It didn't take long and once again her bold overconfidence made it easy. Alone in a boxy Jeep decades past its prime, she drove right by him.

He groaned when he spotted the temporary license plate and his hopes for a name and registration evaporated.

A little voice in his head told him this was too easy, she was practically daring him to follow. But she was a breadcrumb, and possibly the last good lead he'd get today. There was nothing to do but stay on her tail as she took the ramp and joined the sparse traffic traveling toward the mountains.

Fortunately her vehicle was distinctive enough he could fall back to the limits of visibility and still follow. There were several places she might be headed, but this was the most direct route to the area where Director Casey was supposed to be.

Observe and report might be his orders, but he reviewed his tactical options anyway as they inched along. He kept the radio on, listening for any update on the explosion at the airport. A report of a traffic tie-up on the east side of Denver distracted him. The reporter announced a hit-and-run combined with unconfirmed reports of gunfire.

Jason didn't know the city well enough to attribute that

event to his assignment or more localized violence. The roads were treacherous and even driving cautiously he could feel the tires sliding over patches of ice. Using the voice control on his phone, he contacted the analyst again to ask about the traffic report.

He heard the soft tap of fingers on a keyboard before the voice filled the car. "Traffic cameras confirm the report of a collision and it looks to me like there's a muzzle flash."

He asked for, and received an accurate description of the vehicles involved. "Did the police take anyone into custody?"

"Negative. Cameras show the SUV leaving the scene and two men exiting the disabled sedan."

"Anything odd reported?"

"The two men in the sedan left the weapons behind. I can check with the lab about fingerprints, but it won't be the priority with no victims."

"Any chance of facial recognition on anyone from the traffic cams? License plates or registrations?"

"Possibly the driver of the SUV." The soft sound of fingers on the keyboard was all he heard for a moment. "The rest were camera-shy and I don't have enough to go on. Both vehicles are rentals and I can call you back when the records come through."

"Do that. Please," he added. "Is the SUV driver a man or woman?"

"Woman."

DeRossi. "Any GPS signal on the SUV?"

"No."

Jason stifled his exasperation. "The director didn't happen to call in about this same accident, did he?"

"No word from him since he landed safely in Denver."

Jason muttered an oath and thanked the analyst. "Let me know when you get a match on the driver."

"Will do."

"One more thing." Jason gave the temporary tag on the Jeep. "I don't expect the information to be accurate, so dig deeper than the first name that shows up."

"You got it."

When the call disconnected, he pounded his palm against the steering wheel. Of all the times to slip up. Losing DeRossi was the biggest mistake he'd made since becoming a Specialist.

He urged his car closer to the battered Jeep, determined to confirm how the sexy redhead fit in with DeRossi and the director, or if his instincts were all wrong and he was out here chasing wild geese through a blizzard.

Chapter Five

Clutching the steering wheel, Jo's knuckles were as white as the snow outside and, despite the heat blasting from the vents, probably as cold.

She merged with the westbound traffic, praying they would make it to the cabin she'd rented before the police caught up with them. Living in a wired society made it difficult to operate under the radar. Training helped, as did the ultimate clearance level she'd earned by working oversight for the most covert government agencies.

After driving for a few miles encountering nothing more exciting than a snow plow, she tried to relax a fraction and sort out their options. When she trusted her voice again, she asked Thomas who and what he'd seen in the other car.

"A silencer."

"Really?" Not much reason for a silencer in a car chase.

"It doesn't make sense to me either."

"Unless they planned to take you down at the airport."

"I thought that was your job."

She flexed her hands on the wheel, anything to ease the tension. "Is the wedding important to you?"

"You know it is."

"Think what a crushing blow it would be for the bride if her uncle couldn't make it because he was dead."

She felt his hard stare. "When did Initiative launch an assassination division?"

"It's not like we don't have the resources," she said, completely irritated with the bitterness she heard in his voice.

"I'm holding a gun and a sedative, Johara."

"And I'm in the driver's seat of a perfectly effective weapon, too, Thomas." She jumped at his sudden bark of laughter. "How is that funny?"

"Not funny. Absurd." He made a show of lowering the weapon, but she wasn't sure where he'd hidden the sedative disk. "Whatever this is about, I can't believe you're ready to sacrifice yourself. Just level with me. I am completely out of patience."

It was her turn to laugh. "As if you ever had any. You've never been anything less than ironclad."

At one time she'd thought there'd been something underneath all that stoic determination and razor-sharp intelligence. Something closer to personal concern and compassion—maybe even something that could turn into love—but she'd been wrong.

Still, they had a history and more than that, her professional respect for him had never faltered. This investigation was nothing more than an elaborate attempt to discredit him. It had to be. He'd made some impossibly difficult choices in his career, but she would never believe he was a traitor. No matter what the anonymous informant said, if Thomas was here to sell a deadly virus, there would be a legal, big-picture reason for it.

"Seems to me you're holding up well enough. You eliminated that threat quickly enough."

"I'll take that as a compliment and not as some insinuation that I staged a road rage incident." She reached into her purse and withdrew a map. One of the first things she'd done after renting this car was disable the GPS so the rental agency couldn't track her down. She wasn't about to use a computerized navigation system that logged her progress turn by turn.

"Would you navigate please?" She handed the map to him. "I'd like to get off the main roads."

"The side roads will be in worse condition."

"I'm aware of that. But they're less likely to be monitored. Our destination is circled in red."

"Mmm-hmm. And you circled Glenstone Ski Lodge in blue. Why is that?"

"Good skiing."

"You're not making it any easier to trust you."

"I've saved your life a couple times over in the last hour."

"Or you've perfectly executed an intricate setup."

"Hardly." He wouldn't say that if he'd known about the lingerie she'd added to her suitcase at the last minute… just in case they managed to find time to indulge in another sexy rendezvous. She was tempted to tell him about the sheer black lace just to test his reaction, but she kept her mouth shut because she didn't trust her response. This torch she carried for him should have burned out by now and it bothered her knowing she couldn't seem to get over him, though the lingering affection was clearly one-sided.

"Take this exit and turn left at the end of the ramp."

She followed his instructions, wondering if he would mislead her and try to escape. Best to nix that now. "The fact of the matter is you have the gun and the sedative because I want you to have them."

His doubt came through loud and clear and he didn't have to say a word.

Her statement might not be entirely true as it applied to

the sedative, but she refused to back down. "I need you to trust me, even if you don't trust the committee."

"*You* are synonymous with the committee."

"Are you still bitter about that inquiry last year?"

Again, his silence was answer enough.

"That wasn't my idea. It was a supply audit, for Pete's sake. Nobody was going to reprimand you for having one too many sniper scopes." His department had been the only one to show a balanced inventory sheet, but she wasn't inclined to share that detail with him.

"Whose idea was it?"

"The audit?" She caught his affirmative nod out of the corner of her eye. "It's random. The computer spits out a list periodically and we follow through."

"Then there are fewer shadow agencies than I suspected."

She wasn't about to take that bait. "What do you mean?"

"That was our second supply audit in as many years. At the time I assumed your committee had lost something valuable and didn't know where else to look."

For the first time since she'd intercepted him at the airport, she felt like she'd made the right call. He was making her think about the situation from other angles.

"What 'something valuable' would the Initiative have to lose?" she ventured. Besides operatives. Burnout was a frequent problem for agents in her position. It wasn't easy being the pariah of the intelligence community. Even when no one in the public sector knew you existed. Being known to and despised by your peers posed a definite challenge and very few people dealt with it well.

"You'd know that answer better than I would, Jo."

She opted to explore a different theory. "Tell me how Mission Recovery handles discipline problems."

"Why?"

"Humor me. We've got hours ahead of us at this pace." The storm was playing havoc with her timeline. Snails could tour entire gardens in the time it took them to reach the next turnoff as they drove west toward the mountains.

"We select our agents specifically to avoid discipline problems."

"That's a nice party line, Director. I'm completely sold. Now tell me what you do when a good agent screws up."

"You're the oversight genius. You know the routine."

"Actually, I don't. There isn't a single shred of information about how you handle problem children."

"Because we haven't had any," he insisted. "If you're after a specific person or case, just say so."

"Fine." She was after the needle in the haystack and hoping maybe a disgruntled candidate who'd been turned down for a spot on the elite team might be causing trouble for Thomas. "I'm fishing here, there's no specific person I can point to and say 'he or she started this.'"

"Which leaves a specific case."

Naturally, Thomas would hear the details she'd left out.

"Possibly." But her mind was turning over the audit wrinkle. Two supply-specific audits in the same number of years didn't feel random. Annual reports were usually verified by an accountant and approved, unless there was a significant discrepancy. "Did the same person oversee both of your audits?"

"Don't you know the answer to that?"

She didn't want to admit only the most recent audit was on the system. Another reason she'd been surprised. "Contrary to popular belief, I have other things on my daily agenda beyond the shadowy workings of Mission Recovery."

"I'm so relieved."

She resisted the urge to snap at him. Keeping her voice light, she repeated her question about the auditors.

"Two different people, neither of whom I've seen before or since."

And he would have been looking. She didn't believe people who inconvenienced Thomas would ever be welcome in his offices and state-of-the-art training facility without his express permission. On the plus side, there weren't that many people with the committee's authority. It should be easy enough to track down those records and examine the personnel jackets of the auditors involved.

"I think we should stop soon," Thomas said. "You're nearly out of gas."

She glanced down and frowned at the gauge. "The tank was full when I parked it at the airport."

"Roll down your window," he said, powering down his own.

The moment she did the strong smell of gas came in with the blowing snow and wind. "Damn it. A lucky bullet left them a trail." She had a terrible action-movie image of someone tossing a match into the trickle of gas they were leaking and succeeding in blowing them up this time.

"In better conditions maybe," he said. "I never thought I'd be thankful for nasty weather. The snow will blur our trail, but I don't see how we'll make it to wherever this is," he said, tapping the red circle on the map.

"With a leaking gas tank I don't see how we'll make it much of anywhere," she grumbled.

"Just roll into the next convenience store and I'll see what I can do."

"I'm fresh out of duct tape." There were few things in life she hated more than looking incompetent. Looking incompetent in front of Thomas Casey was one of them.

Spotting the faint glow of neon signs up ahead, she prayed for a way to salvage the situation.

"Good thing you've got me then," he remarked without glancing her way. "Park over there." He pointed to a spot away from the security camera aimed at the main door. "Got a flashlight?"

She shook her head. "I'll go buy one."

"Let me go in and ask. You stay with the car and sit tight."

Tight was easy to manage with her current stress level. It made sense not to leave the vehicle unattended, despite the low risk of someone managing to track them through the storm, but she couldn't sit here and do nothing. She got out of the car, wrapped in Thomas's overcoat once more. Underneath the lingering acrid stench of the explosives, she caught the woodsy scent of his cologne. It was almost as good as being in his embrace.

Foolish, but she took comfort in it anyway. When they'd worked in Germany, she'd been his contact and part of his cover. He'd been her rock, her anchor. At the time, she thought she'd done well enough to have been a steadying force for him, too. But the moment they'd returned to the States and debriefed the mission, he'd disappeared from her life.

She hadn't seen him again until official business between the Initiative committee and his Mission Recovery division put them in the same small conference room deep inside the Pentagon one day. That had been more than two years ago and, fool that she was, she'd expected him to call.

Walking around the car, looking for damage, she pushed those sweet memories aside and searched for more pertinent details on the current predicament. Starting with his coat. She patted pockets inside and out, but came up empty. If he was here to sell a vial of a deadly virus, surely he'd keep it on him.

Whoever was tailing them had the skill and audacity to act quickly. It eroded her peace of mind, created a level of doubt that would swell into full-blown panic if she let it. As careful as she'd been, she'd only spotted Specialist Grant in the days preceding Thomas's arrival in Denver.

Nothing in his personnel record indicated dissatisfaction to the point of blowing up the director, but she was fresh out of other theories. It was hard to imagine another team watching her closely enough to take that kind of action and yet hide so effectively that she missed them. And why wouldn't a team targeting both of them wait a few more seconds until they were both in the car? And why didn't the enemy just shoot them when the bomb missed?

There were no easy answers. There wouldn't be until she could get Thomas to trust her enough to cooperate. This whole investigation had felt off since she first got wind of it back in D.C. As uncomfortable as it would be, as vulnerable as it would make her and the committee, it was time to tell Thomas everything. She didn't see another way to determine which of them was the real target and which was convenient collateral damage.

As she came around the back end of the car, she shivered. Not from cold. From the realization someone had marked her rental. No way the small hole drilled into the taillight was a mistake or the result of her evasive maneuvers. Too clean for a bullet, the precise hole in the red plastic brake light made the SUV easy to spot from a distance.

Damn. She should have noticed this at the airport. She might have if her ears and the rest of her senses hadn't been overloaded by the near-miss explosion and desperation to get to safety.

And the sounds and scents of having *him* so close.

Where the hell was he? The idea that he could be in there making a call…deciding he couldn't trust her—

"You shouldn't be out here in heels," Thomas said, joining her. "You'll break an ankle."

She appreciated the concern, but the shoes were trashed anyway and the heels were the only thing keeping her feet out of the deepening snow. There must be two fresh inches on the ground already. "I'll change in a minute."

"Change?"

"I put a backup kit in both cars," she admitted. She just didn't feel inclined to tell him where the other car was.

He rolled his eyes and she knew he was thinking about what the authorities would find when they combed through the wreckage of the car bomb.

"But no snow boots?"

"Cut me some slack. The weathermen didn't even see this coming. It's October. Cold is one thing, a foot of snow is another."

"I know, I know." He waved the flashlight. "Let me see what this gas leak looks like." He knelt down, peering under the car to examine the damaged gas tank.

She thought she should help him somehow, but her knowledge and experience were lacking when a problem was more involved than checking the oil or changing a tire. Give her any sort of weapon and she was good. Analyzing or repairing a vehicle, not so much. Still, she tried, scanning for damage on the body in the vicinity of the fuel tank.

"Not a bullet," he reported, getting to his feet. "Must have been damaged by debris from the collision. I'll find something to patch it up."

"You can do that?"

"Yes," he said blowing into his hands to warm them. "It's our best option."

She'd been debating and discarding other transportation options. It didn't seem likely they would be able to get a cab to pick them up in these conditions.

"Wait in the car. We don't need to add frostbite to our list of problems."

"Yes, sir." She wasn't really offended by the way he snapped orders. This was Director Casey on the job. Any doubts she'd entertained about him lowering his guard or being more relaxed considering the purpose of his travel plans were gone.

From the driver's seat she watched the minutes tick by on the dashboard clock, wondering what was taking him so long. Every moment they weren't moving away from Denver was an opportunity for their enemy to gain ground. Apparently the director's arrival wasn't any more of a secret than his destination.

When he finally emerged, a plastic shopping bag in one hand and a red plastic gas can in the other, she hurried out to join him. "How can I help?" Anything to get them on the road faster.

"Go change your clothes," he said with a scowl. "That uniform is too memorable." He set the gas can and bag on the ground.

"Did you notice if they have any red cloth or tape?" She tapped the damaged light.

"So that's how they picked us up so fast in the city."

"It must be."

Thomas rubbed her arms briskly then nudged her toward the car. "I'll be finished here in a few minutes."

"Then we keep moving." Her emphatic nod lost a little something with her chattering teeth.

"Then we keep moving." With a grim expression, he set the gas can and bag on the ground and crept under the car again.

While he dealt with the gasoline tank, Jo crawled into the backseat and reached over for the small duffel bag she'd left there.

In the near dark, with snow falling in bigger flakes against the window, she almost missed the flutter of paper. On her knees, she leaned over the seat and reached for the small square.

It was more than paper, it was money. Her fingers recognized the feel even as she unfolded it. She snapped on the dome light to get a better look. It was a fifty-euro note. The serial number on the note told her it was issued by Germany. But it was the other ten digits hand-printed on the short end that stirred her curiosity. She recognized the first three numbers as a Washington, D.C. area code, but the rest of what appeared to be a phone contact was unfamiliar to her. On reflex, she reached toward her purse for her cell, eager to see who picked up on the other end. If this actually was a phone number. Then she remembered Thomas had tossed her phone into the fiery remains of the SUV.

The blizzard seemed warm in comparison to the sudden chill seeping into her bones.

She pulled a change of clothing out of the duffel, but her mind was on the money and how anyone had slipped it into her car. She jumped when Thomas opened the driver's door.

"I'm finished," he said, that frown still tugging at his brow.

"That was quick," she said with a smile that did nothing to ease his expression. The man was too observant for his own good.

"It was a relatively easy fix." He held up the gas can. "I'll go pump a couple of gallons into the container and we'll see if it holds up. Are you okay?"

"Fine," she fibbed. "Just cold."

"All right. It might be smart to turn off the light before you change clothes."

He closed the door and she sagged against the seat. Her survival instincts warred with the decision to simply tell him everything, or hold back the more sensitive details. There was no better ally than Thomas Casey, but no worse enemy. She just couldn't be sure how he'd react.

Continuing her mental debate, she shimmied out of her skirt and pulled her jeans on over her hose. More layers would be welcome in this weather. Next, she swapped her blazer for a hooded sweatshirt emblazoned with the Air Force Academy logo. She was reaching for hiking boots when the door opened again.

"The repair looks good. I'm going to move the car and fill it up."

"Great." She told herself she'd feel better, steadier, when they reached the cabin.

"When was the last time you slept? You're pale."

Did the man have to comment on every little thing? "I got six straight hours last night. Anyone would be pale after our recent troubles." *Anyone but him, apparently.*

He moved the car, braved the elements once more to pump the gas. Through the window, she watched him chafe his hands while the machine did the work. Tying her shoes, she grabbed his overcoat and slid out the opposite side of the car. She rounded the hood, brushed more snow off the headlights and handed him his overcoat.

"Put this on. I'm just running inside for a couple of things."

"Hurry. Camera is at ten o'clock. Keep your head down."

She gave him a mock salute and shuffled through the snow to the store. Grabbing a couple of soft drinks, a bag of chips, two pairs of gloves and two stocking caps, she waited for the gas pump to finish and paid cash for the total.

Wishing the clerk a safe evening, she opened the door only to find Thomas had moved the car so she wouldn't have to traipse through the snow again.

"Thanks," she said boosting herself into the passenger seat. She made quick work of the seat belt and, as he put the car in gear, she took the labels and price tags off of the gloves. "Put these on."

"The heater's going now."

"So I'm late with the thoughtfulness. Can't hurt."

He tugged the gloves on one by one and continued the slow drive to the cabin she'd prepared.

"Do you need directions?"

"I memorized the route," he replied.

Of course he did. And probably a backup route, too. "Are you worried they'll pick us up again?"

"Aren't you?"

"A little, yes." The drilled taillight and the marked currency made her wonder what else the people setting up Thomas might have done. What else they might know. Too bad she hadn't thought to pack a signal jammer. "Does it even matter?"

"It matters to me."

"Sorry. I was thinking out loud."

He turned the wiper blades to high and adjusted the defrost setting. "May as well share."

"I was scolding myself for not packing a signal jammer and wondering, based on our circumstances, if it would have made any difference."

His shoulders hitched. "Fair question."

"Does this number mean anything to you?" she read off the phone number.

"What kind of paper is that?"

"It's a euro. I recognized the country of origin by the serial number. Germany."

He didn't say anything else, and he had that famous inscrutable expression on his face, but she felt the tension radiating off of him. She shouldn't read much into the reaction. For all she knew the storm and lack of visible road signs were getting under his skin.

"Where did the euro come from?"

"Someone left it in the car. The locked car. Right on top of my duffel bag to be precise."

"Theories?"

"I haven't had a lot of time to work up any theories," she admitted.

"You've got time now."

Based on his reaction, and the way he diverted the topic, she had to assume he recognized the number. Would that be a benefit or a hindrance moving forward?

"Theory number one, the one that brought me out here this weekend, is that someone is here in Denver gunning for you."

He snorted. "That's not a theory, it's a fact. Someone somewhere is always gunning for me."

His stomach tightened at the truth she already knew. "I'm sure, but who really knows how to find you?"

"The Initiative," he said with bitter intensity.

"That's your theory. And it's flawed because whether you believe me or not, I am on your side."

"That's just one of my theories." He squinted out at the road again. "There's something else on your mind."

"Theory two is *I've* been set up by someone and making you look bad is a convenient bonus."

"Cross me off the suspect list." He swore, checked the rearview mirror and backed up to make the turn he'd missed. "I haven't thought about you in years."

"Oh, stop. Such praise will go straight to my head." She cursed herself for feeling those words all the way to her bones.

"Truth hurts sometimes."

It might hurt more if she believed it. Yes, he'd walked away from the leading edge of a relationship she thought had great potential. His reasoning had been clear from the beginning of their time together. His work wasn't just important to him, it had global implications. Being involved with someone, caring about them, gave the enemy an easy target.

The very act of staying unattached told her just how important she was to him. How important she had been at one time, anyway.

As a member of the small, shadowy community of intelligence agencies she understood his concerns completely. It was no coincidence she'd adopted his philosophy and avoided lasting personal relationships when she landed her current post.

"We could always go with the classic theory that it's all a bad dream," she offered, trying to lighten the mood. The fact was at this point, with a blizzard interrupting communication, theories and educated guesses wouldn't help them much.

"I could get behind that one. But my cold, wet feet and ruined shoes are proof enough of an annoying reality for me. I don't suppose you packed anything in my size."

"Not in the car, no."

"Because you expected me to be unconscious?"

"It might have been a contributing factor." A dreadful thought occurred to her. "Your tuxedo for the wedding wasn't in your suitcase, was it?"

"No. It was delivered directly to the resort."

"Finally something is going our way."

He slid a dubious glance at her. "You can't really expect me to believe the wedding is a primary goal for you."

"It's important to you, so it's important to me that we get you there in one piece."

"Does anyone know about your hideaway?"

"Anyone?"

"Don't be obtuse, Jo. You know what I'm asking."

"No one at work knows. I rented it with my mother's maiden name."

"That's an easy enough personal detail to uncover. Please tell me you didn't search for the property or call the agent from your office?"

"No," she said though gritted teeth. "I'm not a fool. I picked up the assignment and developed a plan of action based on the information and implications."

"What are the implications?"

"Bogus. Dangerous. That's why I'm here." If Thomas Casey was a traitor, she'd tender her resignation as soon as the weather cleared. "We learned about the outbreak, discovered the virus you recovered from the Germany mission is missing and..." Her voice trailed off. It made her sick just to think it. She didn't want to say it aloud.

"And?"

She swallowed, but it did nothing to clear the bad taste from her mouth caused by the outrageous accusation. "And received an anonymous tip that you plan to sell another vial of the virus while you're here for the wedding."

"Any kind of confirmation on that tip?" His quiet tone did nothing to dull the lethal edge behind the question.

"Your supposed buyer has been in the country for several months with a diplomatic detail."

"Whose diplomatic detail?"

Inside she cringed. "I was told I didn't need to know. However, four weeks ago with the support of U.S. officials, the criminal known as Whelan entered the country to assist with the takedown because he claims he can identify the buyer."

"Convenient excuse." Thomas flexed his hands on the steering wheel.

His reaction worried her. She'd heard the rumors about his history with Whelan, but her search for accurate details had come up empty. Considering the close call at the airport, her personal vendetta theory was gaining traction. But that didn't explain away the outbreak or the potential virus sale. "The agency that arranged for his assistance needs the deal to go through so they can arrest both the seller—you—and the buyer."

Expecting an outburst, an immediate protest or at least another question, she found his prolonged silence at that revelation unnerving. She knew he was processing, had been trying to figure the angle on all of this since she led him away from his anticipated wedding agenda.

He downshifted to get up the next hill. "So the armchair quarterbacks and their perfect hindsight vision have decided to dig my grave, literally and figuratively, when I'm distracted with my niece's wedding. That's cold. Even for the Initiative."

"As a committee we are *not* behind this."

"Says the woman who doesn't know the source."

"I admit that looks bad, but I purposely took this on in order to protect you and prevent what looks to me like a more personal vendetta."

"Protect me," he muttered. "From the Initiative or from something else?"

How to tell him? How was less important than what, she decided, and sharing what she knew might help him trust her faster.

"My committee received intel that you already sold the

virus to one extremist group and this new buyer is a line back into the Isely family."

"Bull. We eliminated them as a player five years ago. That was the whole point of the Oberammergau mission. It was considered a successful takedown."

"I remember." *All too well.* She remembered the bruises and burns on his body when he'd made it—two hours late—to the rendezvous point. She'd driven through the night across the mountain and into Austria while he pretended he wasn't wounded. He'd joked about padding the expense account when she checked into the most extravagant hotel in the area.

She remembered turning up the music on the radio as she dug a bullet out of his back, the marble and mirrors of the luxurious bathroom serving as cold, silent witnesses. It hadn't made the task easier. If she closed her eyes, she could still see the bright red trickle of his blood swirling in the drain of the white porcelain bathtub.

"Which is why I'm here. Someone thinks they are back in business. I thought you might take the news better from me."

"Who's the source? What are your orders?"

"As I said, the source was need-to-know, but I was assured the information is verified and legitimate."

He swore. She couldn't blame him; she felt the same way working in the dark like this. "My thinking was we'd review who had the most to gain from this kind of allegation and trace it backward to the real source."

He was quiet a long time, focused on the slippery roadway she assumed, as they slogged up the mountain toward the cabin.

"How can you run any sort of valid investigation if you don't have all the facts?"

"Come on, Thomas, you already know the answer. We

work in the shadows and follow orders. If you have facts to share, I'm all ears."

She wasn't sure if it was the lousy condition of the road or the fading adrenaline, but Thomas didn't seem eager to give her any reply. Pushing him felt counterproductive, so she used the silence to pray they could figure this out before his enemies caught up with them.

Chapter Six

Glenstone Lodge, 7:00 p.m.

Victoria Colby-Camp looked out over the muted landscape that fell away from the wide windows of the chalet resort. In just a few short hours, what had been a stunning view full of color had turned into something more appropriate for the monochromatic beauty of an Ansel Adams exhibit.

"We certainly went from autumn to winter in record time." She couldn't help being in awe of nature's power. "It only adds to the beauty up here."

"I doubt anyone trying to drive through it would agree with you," her husband noted.

She thought of his car accident during a case in Texas and rubbed the resulting chill from her arms. "Lucas, you said Thomas would stay in Denver tonight." She hoped he wouldn't attempt reaching the lodge in this weather.

"And he will. Don't worry about him, he's safe. You look lovely." He kissed her softly, and her heart fluttered. Even after all these years his touch thrilled her. "Almost perfect."

"Almost?" She caught the teasing tone and leaned back, wondering what he had up his sleeve.

He drew a slim, velvet box from his jacket pocket. "Something to commemorate the occasion."

"Occasion?"

"An entire resort full of friends who have become our family? There have been plenty of our investigators who've married, but this feels like a milestone. The interlinking of the very best, the Colby Agency and the CIA, with the solemn vows of marriage."

"Hmm. I could get used to this." Victoria opened the box and couldn't suppress a sigh. "Oh, Lucas, it's gorgeous." Sapphires sparkled among diamonds in a gleaming platinum setting. "Help me put it on. My hands are shaking."

"You're steady as a rock about everything else," he said with a smile.

"I'm entitled to a weakness." She kissed him. "Or two."

They left their suite to join the party downstairs, meeting Ian and Nicole Michaels at the elevator. Ian had long been Victoria's second-in-command at the Colby Agency. He had been at her side almost from the beginning.

"This was the best idea," Nicole said to Victoria while they waited. "Every room has an amazing view. We saw some deer out near the trees before the storm rolled in. The children were ecstatic."

The four of them boarded the elevator and Victoria's heart was full seeing the people she cared about most so happy and content. Though her agency worked hard to be the best in the business of private investigations, Lucas was right: these people were their family.

"It may be a wedding party," Ian said with a wink for his wife, "but this kind of snowfall requires more than a mere snowball fight. I'm going to have the groom add an all-out war to tomorrow's schedule."

"Choose sides carefully," Nicole threatened. "I think the bride has the groom wrapped tightly around her little finger. Levi may not be entirely dependable."

"What do you think?" Ian looked to Lucas. "Boys against the girls?"

The elevator doors parted. "Only if you're prepared to lose."

Nicole elbowed her husband. "Now *there* is an intelligent man."

Victoria smiled. It wasn't often the Colby family, much less anyone from the CIA and its Mission Recovery team, could just relax and enjoy.

As they entered the great room, Victoria's breath caught. The decorator had outdone himself. Despite the rustic lodge setting, the white satin bows and the elaborate flower arrangements added the perfect element of bridal glamour. White candles flickered amid bowls of what looked like pearls. Yet it was the bride and groom-to-be who positively glowed as they chatted with Levi's mother near the massive stone fireplace.

Casey spotted them and hurried over. After a quick hug and an admiring examination of Victoria's new bracelet, she turned to Lucas. "Have you heard from Uncle Thomas?" Her bright smile dimmed just a little. "He hasn't called Mom or me."

"His plane landed on time," Lucas assured her. "He considered hoofing in on a pair of cross-country skis, but I told him to stay in Denver tonight."

"There's an image," Casey said with a quick laugh. "I just expected him to call me when he landed."

Though she doubted anyone else noticed, Victoria saw the brief flicker of surprise in Lucas's eyes.

"With this kind of storm the networks must be swamped and there are probably localized power outages already." Lucas wrapped an arm around the bride's shoulder, guiding her back into the party. "No reason to worry. The roads will be clear enough for him to travel tomorrow."

Casey took a deep breath and smiled as Levi joined them. "Uncle Thomas is safe in Denver," she told her husband-to-be.

"That's great news." Levi was clearly relieved, as well. "The weathercasters say this monster storm will be long gone by our wedding day."

As the delighted couple drifted off to chat with other guests, Victoria gave Lucas a pointed look. He'd gone way overboard in his assurances. Something was up.

"Would you like some wine?"

"Chardonnay, please," she answered. "But that won't distract me from wondering what you're up to."

"Terrible to waste good wine and good company worrying over what can't be changed."

She shrugged a shoulder and turned on a bright smile. "You'll tell me eventually."

Though he'd been surprised by Thomas's lack of communication with his niece, Victoria knew her husband well enough to know he wasn't particularly worried about his friend. Come to think of it, he wasn't the sort of man one worried about. Thomas Casey was James Bond personified. There was little he couldn't overcome with a roll of duct tape and a toothpick.

Lucas cleared his throat. "In the meantime, we're snowbound in a beautiful chalet with good food and people who love each other. I, for one, intend to enjoy it thoroughly."

With a glass of wine in her hand, Victoria visited with the bride's mother, listened to the bride and bridesmaids' adventures in shopping and planning for the big day and kept a keen eye on her husband.

She wasn't sure if she should be grateful or worried for the storm's interference with the cell service. It was nice to relax and focus on the life and promise bustling around her, but semi-retirement or not, she was accustomed to staying in contact with the world.

When the resort opened up the dining room for dinner, Lucas appeared at her side. As with the rest of the arrangements and activities so far, everyone seemed delighted and happy. Again, the decorations were well-done. The lovely touches of white reflected the winter wonderland outside.

Victoria was pleased to see Casey and Levi relaxed, but she caught the telltale look in her husband's eyes. "You're thinking about Thomas."

"Only that it's a shame he's stuck in a hotel room missing this."

"Well, the food is definitely better than any room service he might order tonight."

"So's the Scotch," Lucas said with a wave of his glass. "How is the bride?"

"I'd say she's managing her nerves. Levi and her friends are keeping her distracted. Her mother is steady as ever."

"She's had a lifetime of practice waiting out unexpected delays first with her own work as well as her husband's in the CIA, not to mention her brother, Thomas. Raising a daughter determined to follow in their footsteps and now having to handle all this without Casey's father."

It had been a year since Casey's father died but Victoria felt sure it wasn't easy to be the mother of the bride without her lifelong partner. She took a sip of her wine. "I've always thought weddings are just a shade easier for a groom's mother. For Casey and her mother's sake, I hope Thomas gets here first thing in the morning."

"I can't imagine he'll waste any time," Lucas said. "Walking her down the aisle might make him nervous, but only in the best possible way."

Victoria smiled, anticipating the wedding. "It's sure to be a memorable moment for all of us."

Chapter Seven

Jason spent another thirty minutes tailing the Jeep, while he waited for word from the office. Naturally, there were plenty of places she might be headed, but he just didn't believe she was going anywhere other than Glenstone.

The blizzard was getting worse and he knew better than to miss the next check-in, or worse, have no new intel on DeRossi when he called.

He had the woman's photograph and the information on the temporary license plate. It would have to be enough for now. Resigned and frustrated, he took the next exit and headed back to Denver and DeRossi's hotel.

Orders or not, there was no way he would sit back and allow open season on Director Casey to go unanswered. The man had done too much for Jason, personally and professionally.

He turned up the volume on his phone and opened the police scanner app in case they got into some new trouble.

The director was more than a boss or mentor; the man never asked his Specialists to do more than he himself was ready to do. Lessons and memories flashed through his mind as he battled the weather to get back across town.

Nearing the airport, he dialed DeRossi's hotel and asked for her room number. When no one picked up, he ended the call and then dialed her official cell number. That call went straight to voice mail and Jason hoped it meant his search of her room wouldn't get interrupted.

He found a parking space that afforded a quick exit if necessary and braced for the long walk through the bitter weather. Cold and wet, the warmth of the lobby was a welcome relief. He brushed the snow from his hair and rubbed the chill from his hands as he strolled toward the main elevators. He pressed the button for the floor above DeRossi's and, knowing how to blend in, he chatted about the unexpected weather with the other guests who boarded the car.

When the elevator stopped at his floor, he exited and deliberately took the long way around toward the stairwell nearest the service areas. It took him a few minutes, but he found a maid with her cart and gave a room number. He sweet-talked her out of extra towels, while pocketing her key card, then headed for the stairs.

Down one flight, towels under his arm, he moved quickly to DeRossi's room. He knocked, paused, then swiped the card through the reader.

His gaze swept the room, taking in details with one swift glance. She'd left clothes on hangers, and the luggage rack was out, but there wasn't any luggage in the room. He spotted a cell phone charger in the outlet by the desk, but the tablet he'd seen her use at lunch yesterday wasn't here. Everything pointed to her intention to return, so he quickly searched for any clues about why she had intercepted the director.

"What do you know that I don't?" He whispered the question into the empty room as he opened drawers, peeked under both mattresses and searched in and around the mini fridge and microwave.

Finding two wigs explained how she'd slipped by him, and it made him feel all the more determined to find something relevant now.

He paused, hands on hips, feeling every second tick by. Holt wanted to know what DeRossi knew and Jason couldn't imagine admitting another failure today. The main area of the room was clean so he moved toward the bathroom and vanity, mentally crossing his fingers he'd find something to report.

All of the places he would have hidden something vital were empty. He worried someone might have beaten him to the search, but the room was so clean there was no way to tell. The stunning redhead he'd run into twice already popped into his mind and he pulled a penlight out of his inner pocket. Turning it on, he scanned the room for any sign of her, but came up empty. Jason shook his head. Finding a stray red hair was a long shot and he had to quit following tangents and find something worthwhile for Holt.

He knelt down and peered at the underside of the sink and swore at the flap of tape hanging down.

Surely there had been a more infuriating assignment in his past, but he was hard pressed to remember it right now. He stood up, searched the pockets of the clothing she'd left behind, but there was nothing.

DeRossi had proven more of a challenge than he'd anticipated, and it only put his instincts on high alert. The cosmetic case on the vanity was the only item left he hadn't examined and, with hope dwindling, he poked through it.

Beauty tools, small pots and tubes in various colors and a fabric headband did nothing to shed light on her purpose with the director.

He was running out of time. Any minute the maid would

report her key card missing and a few basic questions would have the security team searching for him.

Frustrated, he checked his reflection in the mirror, tucked away the penlight and smoothed his suit jacket. What had he expected? A detailed outline of her plans signed by De-Rossi lying on the desk?

He was reaching for the door when it hit him. Turning back to the vanity, he went through the cosmetic case once more, confirming what wasn't there. No toothbrush or toothpaste.

"Well, well."

She might have a reservation for this room through Monday, but she had something else planned between now and then.

The second examination of the cosmetic bag proved more valuable as he spotted a tube he'd assumed was just a different brand from the rest of her cosmetics. No, this wasn't a lipstick, it was a flash drive.

He might not know exactly where she was going, but he was finally getting somewhere. Provided this wasn't just a collection of her favorite photos. And it was a relief to know he wouldn't be wasting time loitering in the lobby for her return.

Re-energized, he glanced through the peephole. Seeing no activity in the hall, he pulled the door open a crack and then slipped out. Keeping his head down, he walked toward the opposite stairwell and dropped the key card on his way back down to the lobby.

He reached his rental car without incident and cranked the heater as he called Holt to bring him up to speed.

"Did you find DeRossi and the director?" Holt demanded.

"Not yet, but I know where she isn't."

"Meaning?"

He thought of the flash drive, but didn't want to mention it until he knew it mattered. "Her room is clean, but she's not planning to be back tonight."

"You're sure?"

"Yes." Jason hoped he wouldn't have to explain his certainty.

"Any sign of the problem child?"

"Maybe." For some inexplicable reason, Jason hesitated to mention the explosion or that he'd spotted the redhead there. This was Holt, his boss, trusted as Thomas Casey's second-in-command for years. "DeRossi had a rental car stashed in long-term parking. It was blown up a couple of hours ago. No casualties," he added before Holt could ask.

"Any clues?"

"Nothing substantial yet."

"Stay on it and stay alert."

The line went dead and Jason stared at it for a long moment, a part of him wishing he hadn't passed along that much information.

Something felt off and he just hadn't been able to put his finger on it just yet.

He called around until he found a motel with a vacancy on the west side of town. It was his third room in as many nights and he experienced the rare sensation of wishing for some stability.

As a Specialist his stability was the team, not the location. Sleeping in the same bed two nights in a row had never been that important to him. This was the wrong time to be thinking of anything other than the enigma that was this case.

It took him twice as long as it should have to reach the

place and Jason was thrilled to finally be out of the car. He tossed his bag on the bed and set his laptop on the desk, turning it on. While it booted up, he put the frozen pizza he'd picked up from the kiosk in the lobby in the microwave. Before he left town he vowed to have a thick steak at the best steak house in the city.

He was about to put the flash drive in the port when his cell phone rang. He waited for the second ring to display the caller's information, but the unknown number icon flashed on the screen along with a local area code. "Jason Grant."

"It's Casey."

Adrenaline fired in his veins. "Sir. Are you safe?"

"For the moment, but I haven't reached the resort yet. Agent DeRossi needed to ask me a few questions away from the office."

Jason actively listened for any distress in the director's voice, any clues to his location. It was a relief he sounded at ease, if not relaxed, but he would have preferred some direction.

"Sir, I've been ordered—"

"I'm changing your orders. I need you to pull an immediate background check with last known location and contact on a criminal known as Whelan. Off the record."

Jason wanted to explain his current assignment and give the director some warning but it would have to wait. "Should I report back at this number?"

"No. Send it on to Lucas Camp. He's at the lodge with the wedding party."

"Sir?"

"I'll explain later. This information is only for Mr. Camp."

Jason promised, and surprisingly the director thanked

him before ending the call. He was used to Holt's more abrupt style of barking an order and hanging up before anyone had a chance to ask a question.

Tempted as he was by the flash drive, Jason worked on Whelan's background first. Being a Specialist gave him access to several databases that didn't officially exist, but going through normal channels meant someone would know he'd been poking around.

He didn't think that's what the director had in mind. Whelan was widely known throughout the intelligence community as a creative genius with all things that could catch fire or go boom. He was also known for selling his skills to the highest bidder and he regularly evaded custody and prosecution for his destructive and usually lethal devices.

Jason had only bumped into his work once before. Twice if he counted this afternoon. Assuming the director's inquiry meant he thought Whelan was behind the explosion at the airport parking lot.

Fortunately, he still had discreet friends who could help him learn what Casey needed to know. He winced as he checked his watch and did the math, knowing he'd wake up Brian O'Marron, his pal he'd met during a short stint with Interpol.

He entered the number and waited for it to ring on the other side of the Atlantic. The motel phone would have been more secure, but O'Marron wouldn't bother to answer an unknown caller at this hour. While Mission Recovery analysts might dump his phone logs if things fell apart on this assignment, Jason knew that would take some time. And if questioned, he could offer other valid reasons beyond the director's concerns for making this call. With the phone to his ear, he rubbed his temples trying to get ahead of the tension headache he felt building behind his eyes. This was the safest of his limited options to get the information the director needed.

Provided O'Marron ever answered his damn phone.

After exchanging not-so-pleasant greetings considering the imposition of time, Jason explained his call. "There was an incident today with a car bomb at an American airport."

"Denver," O'Marron said. "I heard."

"Then you're saying he's here?"

His friend went so quiet Jason thought the call had dropped. He held the phone out and verified he still had a signal.

"Were there fatalities?"

"No," Jason replied.

"Then it's bloody well not Whelan."

O'Marron had a point. "Humor me. What do you know about his recent activity?"

"Did you catch the usual signature?"

"No, but it took me a few minutes to get to the scene and the blizzard could have masked that by the time I arrived." The redhead came to mind again. "Has he picked up an apprentice or held a clinic lately?" They both knew he'd done both in the past. The man would do anything for cash.

"Level with me and maybe I'll tell you."

"Keep yanking me around and we'll do this in person."

"As if I can't have you stopped, strip-searched and detained at the border."

Jason laughed. His friend would be surprised when his stunt failed. Mission Recovery had unprecedented credentials and a variety of ways to circumvent that type of power play. "Hospitable as ever. Come on, help me out and I'll owe you one."

"You're confident this is Whelan's work?"

The fact that Director Casey thought so was enough of an endorsement for Jason. "Unless you have intel that says otherwise, yes, I think we can credit him with today's incident."

"Except no one died."

"Come on, O'Marron." Jason bit back the sharp retort. "If you can't give me confirmation, give me something to rule him out. And hurry. I could lose the call any minute with this storm."

"Whelan entered the States four weeks ago, escorted by American authorities."

Which was O'Marron's way of saying it could be anyone from the CIA to Homeland Security who'd extended an engraved invitation to Whelan.

"Where was he before that?"

"Germany, again, but he slipped our net."

"Anything on recent associates?" Like a gorgeous redhead with a killer smirk? The signal popped and crackled, and O'Marron's voice came through in fragments.

"...rumor about a contract...an American agent. Doesn't... stock in that...said they met—"

Jason nearly threw the phone when it showed the signal had been lost. There were too many possible interpretations of those fragments. With a measured sigh he set the phone on the charger. O'Marron had given Jason more than he'd had before. Now he just had to get that information to Lucas Camp.

He turned on the television and scanned the local channels, all of which were reporting on the freak storm. The way this was unfolding, Jason would rather do this face-to-face, but there was no way he'd get up to the Glenstone Lodge tonight in a rented sedan without snow tires.

If the cell towers were out here, chances were good they

weren't working any better in the higher elevations. He picked up the room phone and heard a dial tone.

Hopeful, he drafted a quick note for Lucas, making it as secure as possible under the circumstances, and then he headed down to the front desk.

Chapter Eight

9:05 p.m.

Thomas struggled to ignore the knots in his shoulders and neck while he fought to keep the car on what he hoped was actually the roadway. His hands were cramping and though they weren't going at much more than a crawl, the car's back end kept fishtailing on the tight curves. Yeah, skis would have been the safer bet all around.

He knew Jo wanted answers. It would probably be best if he did open up. He should start with Whelan. Or let her know he'd called a Specialist for an assist. But he wasn't inclined to share the facts about the virus as he currently knew them. Hell, he wasn't sure if he knew anything helpful at all.

Within the offices that didn't officially exist in Washington, he was known for having the intel before anyone else. How had he missed the rumors that prompted the Initiative to launch an investigation against him? He had plenty of enemies, that hadn't been an exaggeration, but he had allies, too. Allies who should have given him some sort of warning this was on the horizon.

He made the last turn and the headlights swept across the snow-covered landscape, bouncing off the fresh blanket of white as he parked in front of the cabin that was their destination. He left the car running and stared through the windshield, weighing the options. It could be a trap, one designed by Jo, or Whelan, or a faceless enemy.

Could he really trust her? Would the smarter choice be to call in and give her as well as himself up?

In a career as blurred by gray-area choices as his had been, every decision came down to one fine point: Would he be able to look at himself in the mirror? This decision was no different, which quickly put an end to his internal debate. He extended his hand. "Give me the key and wait here."

"We'll go in together."

"No."

"I need you to trust me, Thomas."

"Jo, I trust you as much as I trust anyone."

"Well, it's a good thing I know when you're lying to me."

He sighed. She'd always been perceptive and she had the added advantage of having seen him at his worst. Frankly, he was too tired to keep up the facade of a man unperturbed by explosions, gunmen and weather. "The key. Going first shows I trust you not to have something up there rigged to explode or otherwise ruin my night."

"Again, hurting you would be counterproductive to keeping you alive," she grumbled, fishing the key out of her purse.

After giving him a long stare, she handed him the key and he carefully climbed out of the vehicle. The snowfall could very well be hiding trip wires—set by someone other than Jo.

He knew if she wanted him dead, she could have killed him a few different ways by now and saved herself from his increasing irritability. Whether she realized it yet or not, it looked to him like someone was undermining both of them.

Thinking about the phone number on the euro took him back. Way back. And the distinctive citrus scent at the explosion only confirmed his suspicions about Whelan's involvement. Granted, he'd cost the explosives expert a small fortune five years ago, but there had to be a reason he'd make an attempt for revenge now.

The virus rumors, well, that was a bigger concern if the remnants of the Isely family were trying to get back in the bio-weapons game.

He looked around, wondering if they'd been followed. He hadn't seen another car for the past hour, but it paid to be cautious. Behind the car, the snow was already filling in the tire marks. The storm might just help them survive the night. The trees surrounding the cabin were already bowing under the weight of the white covering and he imagined in other circumstances the scene might feel picturesque. In other circumstances they might be a couple on a romantic retreat, rather than two agents running for their lives.

When he reached the porch, he knelt down in the snow and examined each step in the wash of light from the headlights. He was tired and cold, but he ignored both in favor of handling this the right way.

The wind had already created small snowdrifts against the front door and windows. He hoped the owners stored basic tools and supplies for renters. The last thing he needed was to miss the rehearsal dinner because they were snowed in at a remote cabin without any way to communicate with Lucas, or more important, his niece and sister.

His niece was counting on him.

"I will make the wedding," he vowed to the storm as he stood up and braced for the approach to the door.

His feet were nearly numb, but he felt the give of the

first step and waited until he was sure it was just the creaking of old wood and not something more volatile.

"That one is broken," Jo called from the car.

"Thanks for the warning." He climbed the next two with equal caution, just as relieved when he didn't become a bloody impersonation of the car at the airport.

"I'm telling you no one knows about this place," she called out.

"Uh-huh," he muttered.

He knew about it. She knew about it. Whoever had drilled a hole in the taillight might very well know about it.

He stepped toward the door and a loud pop had his heart lodging in his throat. He turned, watching as nothing more dangerous than a breaking branch fell to the ground with a rattle and whoosh.

Damn. He was getting edgier by the second.

Sliding the key into the lock, he murmured a prayer to stay alive just forty-eight more hours. Then the wedding would be over, his family secure and whoever wanted to take their shots could damn well try.

He unlocked the door and withdrew the key. When silence greeted him he thought nothing had sounded sweeter.

Jo came stamping up the stairs behind him, her purse over one arm and her duffel slung across her body. "Told you so."

"You did," he conceded, following her inside and only cringing a little as she flipped on the overhead light.

"Being spooked is understandable," she said, tossing the car keys onto the kitchen counter.

"You do realize being so confident only makes me wonder if you orchestrated the bomb and the car chase along with the rest of this."

"*Not* rehashing that again," she said, hanging his overcoat on a peg by the door. "We both know you believe me."

She untied her shoes and lined them up with the corner of the couch.

He'd forgotten her preference for order in the little things.

"As a general concept maybe."

"Good enough for now. Let's get to work."

"I'll start a fire." Before he couldn't feel his feet at all. Kneeling, he reached in and pulled open the flue. Only a bit of snow fell in and it was soon steaming away as the kindling caught. Standing, he toed off his shoes and shrugged off his suit coat, letting the heat sink in.

"Go on back and get out of those wet clothes," Jo suggested.

"In a minute." He was still braced for the next attack and lounging around in a toga quilt wouldn't leave him feeling empowered.

"Well, at least have a Scotch."

He turned, smiling at the bottle and glass she held out to him. "You remembered."

Five years ago they'd toasted the end of the Isely family in much the same manner after she'd patched him up in a swanky hotel in Austria.

She shrugged. "Maybe. Maybe it was just in your file." She took a slow sip of the two fingers she'd poured for herself and watched him over the rim of her glass.

It probably was in the file. He decided he didn't care. The fire and the Scotch smoothed his ragged nerves and started drawing the tension out of his shoulders.

"I brought some basics for you," she said, not quite meeting his gaze. "Jeans, a sweater and a couple of shirts."

He raised an eyebrow. He wasn't sure he wanted to know how she'd managed that or remembered his size.

"You'll find a small overnight case back in the bedroom."

"Just in case my luggage got blown up?"

Was she blushing or was it the alcohol putting that color in her cheeks?

"I'm embarrassed to say that scenario didn't even occur to me."

"The explosion?" He frowned at her quick nod. "You think it should have?"

"Maybe." She hitched a slender shoulder as she stared into the golden liquid left in her glass. "Get changed. When you see the intel I was given, you can fill in the blanks and tell me if I misinterpreted something vital."

Thinking on that minor revelation, he padded down the short hall toward the light glowing from an open doorway. If Jo had missed something, it would have been the first time.

Her instincts were an asset he'd used to the mission's full advantage in the field. Gazing at the garment bag open on the bed, he realized he'd underestimated her breaking-and-entering skills. She hadn't guessed about his size, it looked like she'd taken clothing straight out of his home. He was more than a little embarrassed he hadn't noticed the missing items and perturbed that she'd found a way past his security system, but at the moment he could only be grateful she'd thought ahead.

Changing into dry clothes, with the Scotch warming him from the inside, improved his mood dramatically.

He returned to the front room to find Jo curled up in a chair by the fire, a quilt over her legs and a tablet in her hands. In the Air Force hoodie, the glow of the screen shining on her face, she looked almost too young to be an accomplished investigator. The fierce attraction he felt to her startled him more than a little. She'd always be beautiful, but wasn't he supposed to be immune after all this time?

"Is there really a wi-fi connection out here?" he inquired.

"Not in this weather," she said with a small frown. "But I have the file here, ready for your review."

"Thanks." He turned toward the kitchen and started poking through the grocery bags on the counter. The fridge was fully stocked, as well. She'd really gone above and beyond.

"What are you doing?"

"Dinner."

"Dinner?"

"Typically the last big meal of the day," he reminded her. "We missed it." He tapped his watch. "Since it seems you were right about us being safe here, I figured we should eat."

"Okay." She unfolded herself from the chair. "But you don't have to cook."

"Now who needs to extend a little trust? I know my way around a kitchen."

"That's not what I meant."

He pulled out a stockpot and saucepan. "May as well whip something up in case we lose power." He filled the stockpot with water and set it on a burner to boil.

"Let me make the salad."

"I'd rather you talked me through whatever it is you know."

"You don't want to read it first? Develop your own opinion?"

He finished pouring the jar of sauce into the smaller pan and set it to warm before turning to face her. "You wanted trust, Jo. I'm here in your cabin, prepping dinner, ignoring the fact that you managed to break into my home." He plucked at the cable knit sweater he'd recently picked up to replace an old favorite.

"Wow." Her eyes went wide with surprise. "If I didn't know better I'd say being director for so long has mellowed you."

"Tell me why you insisted on taking this case and why you think doing so protects me."

"Fine." She squeezed by him and opened the refrigerator, pulling out fresh greens for a salad. "Can you find a bowl, please?"

He opened cabinets until he came up with both a bowl and colander. "Nice place."

"It is."

He watched her work with those slender, deft fingers and tried to forget how they'd once felt on his skin. She would talk eventually, he just had to be patient while she organized her thoughts.

He remembered that about her, too. She wasn't the sort to jump into anything—not a firefight nor a conversation—without thinking it through and weighing the options and potential fallout.

"I'd really like to see the files on the supply audit," she muttered half to herself.

He could make that happen when they had access to the internet, but he kept quiet, not wanting to interrupt her. If she was making a connection there, she'd get to it.

He dumped pasta into the boiling water, added salt and stirred.

"There was an outbreak of a new flu virus two weeks ago in a remote village on the border between Pakistan and Iran."

An icy finger that had nothing to do with the weather system battering the cabin danced across his nape. He recognized the foreboding sense of dread and let it roll on through. Fighting grim emotions wasted energy and he'd long ago learned to channel his energy into appropriate outlets.

"How many dead?"

"Reports were conflicted," she replied, mumbling as she struggled to slice a tomato with what appeared to be a dull knife.

"Does anyone have an eye on Isely Jr.?"

She paused, meeting his gaze from beneath her thick lashes. "I'd hoped you would."

He had little more than a general direction. It had been five years since he'd infiltrated the notorious Isely crime family and botched their sale of a deadly new flu virus. Some had considered the move foolhardy considering his position as director but when he'd escaped the firefight with names, faces, fingerprints of the parties involved, along with the case of vials, he'd considered it a successful mission. Everyone had.

Johara had been his contact and part of his cover story as well as his ticket out of Germany. Riding the high of those few post-mission days, they'd become friends. But after the debriefing stateside, he hadn't seen her again until she'd landed on the Initiative committee.

He'd expected it to stay that way…maybe he'd needed it to. But here they were.

"Those supply audits are starting to make more sense." He'd known they'd been fishing for something. "Someone thinks I have the real virus."

"Don't you?"

"Absolutely not." He tested the pasta, called it al dente and drained the water into the sink.

Conversation stopped until they were settled at the table with the pasta, salad and two bottles of water.

"It's not the Four Seasons," she said with a smile full of tension.

"Does it need to be?"

"No. I just…" Her voice trailed off and this time he knew she wouldn't elaborate.

When they'd last worked together both of them had avoided any talk of feelings. They'd been riding the high of success and indulged the mutual attraction between them. He'd thought living in the moment and taking things one day at a time was best for keeping personal safety and mission integrity a top priority.

Sitting across from her now, as isolated as two people could be, he wondered if he'd been wrong to walk away from her.

Smart, Casey. Go down that path now of all times.

They ate in silence for a few minutes, before she returned to the topic of the investigation.

"From the beginning?" Her eyes were on her plate.

"If that's easier for you," he replied.

"You turned in the vials we brought out of Germany."

"Yes." He twirled another bite of pasta around his fork. "You saw exactly what I brought back. I still carry the receipt they gave me when I handed the case over to the lab."

"Did you know it wasn't a lethal strain?"

"Not until I saw the lab report months later."

"What did you do about it?"

"Do? What could I do? I counted my blessings the chemist screwed up or exaggerated the accomplishment to make the sale to Isely."

He watched her methodically select a bite of salad, but she didn't eat it, just balanced it at the edge of her plate.

"Fair enough. What did you *think* about the chemist's failure?"

"I thought if there really was a lethal strain then Isely had planned all along to double-cross the buyer and keep the real virus for his personal use or a better offer. Doesn't the recent outbreak confirm that?"

"The recent outbreak, and a source who, based on the information, was at the original takedown in Germany, suggests you are the culprit. That you stole and sold the real virus." She took a long drink of her water. "A ridiculous allegation."

"And the Initiative believes that." His stomach clenched. Of course the committee believed an anonymous source over a director with an impeccable record. He had to forcibly relax his jaw. It took him longer than it should have to be able to speak. "Who is the source?"

"There's no name in the file."

He pushed back from the table, unable to sit here and take this anymore. "It's a setup."

"I agree."

"Who hates me that much?"

"After a few years with the committee I can say this sort of vitriol usually comes from an ex-spouse."

"That isn't funny."

"It wasn't meant to be."

"Fine." He held up his hand as if taking an oath. "I don't have a secret wife. You know I never married." And days like this proved why he never should. "Who else even knows me that well?"

"That's what I've been trying to figure out. I took this case to help you prove your years of success as an agent and a director are legitimate."

He spun back to face her. "You mean to tell me a few sick people in the Middle East and a conveniently anonymous source has the committee wanting to dig into all of our cases?"

She nodded. "Sadly, yes. If someone with your authority has sold a bio-weapon they have to consider what other sensitive data might have been compromised within your purview."

"What exactly was your assignment?"

"Exactly?"

He saw her nervous swallow. "Yes."

"Observe the sale of the virus. Then I could intercept you and produce proof of guilt."

"That doesn't sound very impartial."

"Which is why I wanted to handle this case personally."

"Handle me."

"If that's how you want to think of it." Her chin rose in a show of defiance. "Citing my familiarity with the original mission, I told them what they wanted to hear and presented an appropriate plan of action. They gave me the green light."

"To railroad me."

She picked up their plates and moved back to the kitchen. "Someone is gunning for you, yes. I shouldn't have to remind you we work in the gray area, Thomas. I said what needed to be said to position myself between you and the threat."

"Why?" It seemed like a terrible risk personally and professionally. He couldn't fathom her motive. "Why would you do that?"

She scraped the remnants of dinner from their plates into the garbage can. "Because if you'd sold a bio-weapon for personal gain I wanted to be the one to take you out."

He chuckled. "You could try."

"Fortunately we don't need to test it, since you're innocent."

"You're so sure?"

"Yes."

Her unwavering conviction after all this time surprised him. His Specialists had done plenty in that gray area she mentioned. Grabbing a dish towel, he stepped up beside her to dry the dishes as she washed them.

"Then why bring the sedative?" It had been bothering him that she claimed to trust him, yet she'd been prepared to disable him.

She drew her full lower lip between her teeth. "That was just in case they were right."

"A few minutes ago, right there at the table," he jerked his chin in that direction, "you said you didn't believe the allegations."

"Think about it, Thomas. In my place would you have taken the chance?"

"No." He had to let it go. Female agents were trained to take precautions when they were physically outmatched. She'd been honest with him so far, he shouldn't push the issue. He folded the dish towel into smaller and smaller rectangles, opened it up, only to repeat the process. That distinct odor, just before the car blew up, haunted him. He would have been happy to never smell it again. It punctuated his one near failure during the Isely takedown.

"But?" She caught his hands with her smaller ones, stopping the nervous movement.

"But if you had so much confidence in me, were you expecting to need that sedative for someone else?"

Chapter Nine

Johara rolled her eyes and pushed away from the counter. "You still think I hired someone to blow up the car?"

"Didn't you? It certainly forced me to go with you."

"You were already going with me." She folded her arms across her chest and stared him down. "I need you alive. Mission Recovery—good grief, this entire country—needs you alive."

"The entire country doesn't know who I am."

"But someone does know you, Thomas. Or they know what you're capable of. The sooner we figure out who it is, the sooner you'll get to the wedding."

"Show me what you've got."

Finally. She wanted his eyes on the information rather than on her. Those blue eyes made her remember feelings that were best locked away in the corner of her mind. Especially right now. His life—both their lives—depended on finding the truth.

More to the point, he observed and analyzed every nuance, word and gesture. It was as if he were caressing her body with nothing more than that intent gaze. Her body quivered even now.

Focus, Jo. She retrieved her tablet, swiped the screen to pull up the folder and handed it to him. His fingers brushed hers and that heat that kept threatening to devour her fired through her senses yet again. If she survived this night with her head on straight it would be a miracle.

He sank onto the couch as he read, elbows braced on his knees, his eyes never leaving the screen.

In the field, she'd aspired to that same intense focus he gave to every minute of the mission. Not for the first time, she wondered about the men and women on his select team of Specialists. Did they admire him or resent him for being such a hard-ass? She'd only worked with him, not for him. His Specialists didn't complain, but in their line of work everyone had secrets and vulnerabilities. Bottom line, whoever was setting up Thomas had accessed highly classified files with a justified clearance or a talented hacker. No breaches had been reported. To her, that all added up to an inside job.

No one ever wanted that to be the answer.

She might as well be reading over his shoulder; she had the file memorized. From the first memo reporting the odd outbreak, to the intel directly from the "source," to her own notes as she tracked down the current locations of the people involved with the old mission in Germany. She'd cross-referenced the recent travel and connections of those involved five years ago, not coming up with anyone who had traveled to the Middle East. As much as she hated to admit it, she'd hit a brick wall and didn't know how to move forward without Thomas.

When he set the tablet aside and stared into the crackling fire, her patience ran out. "Does it look like someone on the inside to you?"

He pushed a hand over his short-cropped hair and sighed. "You're sure about the statuses on everyone who survived that mission?"

"Yes. Thanks to you there were survivors."

Thomas pointed at the tablet. "Some thanks. Contrary to your opinion, it would seem my country wants me dead." He pushed to his feet. "Okay. Let's go through the paces. Who on our side of the pond has access to Whelan and why would they let him blow up the rental car if what they really want is for me to sell a bio-weapon?"

"He's a mercenary," she said. "He has no allegiance to anyone or any country. From the little I know about Whelan, with enough money and the right advertisement on a leading online classified ads website, he'd meet with anyone."

"Meet him, sure, but we both know that's not what happened. He's been watching you, or getting intel from someone else, knowing when you'd be where."

"The only tail I've seen is your man, Jason Grant."

"I beg your pardon?"

She took two steps back from the deadly quiet tone and hard glare Thomas sent her way. "You didn't know he was here in Denver?"

Thomas shook his head slowly.

"He was at the airport when your flight arrived."

"That's why you hurried us into the employee area."

"Yes."

"And why you asked me about Mission Recovery discipline policy."

"Yes." Before she could ask the next question, Thomas answered it.

"Grant's an exemplary Specialist. I've never had to write up anything but praise for his missions. Holt and I are grooming him to move up when I retire and Holt becomes director."

"I know." At his skeptical look, she explained, "Initiative vetted and approved your choice."

"I feel so affirmed," he said with a small sneer.

She ignored the jab. "Any chance either Holt or Grant wants to hurry you out the door?"

"No. There's no reason, nothing to gain for either of them."

"Power and prestige can be enticing. A little raise in pay grade doesn't hurt either."

He waved her suggestion off like he was swatting a pesky fly. "Grant has a variety of skills, but he's not that good with explosives. He's more of the loner type." She watched him think it through. "He did a stint with Interpol, but I don't think he's good enough to mimic Whelan's signature. Besides, both he and Holt know the additional responsibility comes with additional baggage.

"Look at your own situation," he added. "Moving up the food chain isn't all perks."

She bit back the retort. Arguing about how and why she'd landed the job with Initiative wouldn't help them resolve his predicament and restore his reputation.

"The Initiative believes you've sold out to America's enemies. They won't let go of this bone without hard evidence to the contrary."

"And we both know you can't prove a negative."

He was right. The same thought had been troubling her. "It's a clever trap they're closing on you." She pulled her hair over her shoulder, absently twining it into a braid and unraveling it again.

"There's always a way out. Always a loophole," he said, staring at the fire. "Do you have a burner phone?"

"Not anymore. It was in the suitcase," she explained. "Why?"

"Where's that euro you found?"

"I knew you recognized the number on it." She went to her purse and withdrew the banknote. "Who is it?"

He didn't answer, just turned the euro back and forth then looked at his watch again.

She wanted to ask more questions, to insist he share the information she was sure he was holding back, but she had to be careful not to alienate his limited cooperation. "Are you thinking about Casey?" His niece and sister were here. They could end up targets in this trap, as well.

"No, Holt. We had check-in times scheduled."

"Don't you trust him to handle things while you're away for the weekend?"

"Is that the Initiative asking or the woman stuck in a blizzard with her target?"

Her temper, usually slow to burn, surged like a rocket. She felt her cheeks flush with heat, but she refused to give him the further satisfaction of a verbal outburst. Flipping the braid behind her, she crossed her legs and studied him. She could only hope he'd lose his cool first. "For the last time, this is not an elaborate fishing expedition. What happens here, provided you don't get dead or make contact with a terrorist, stays here."

He stepped closer, doing his best to intimidate her with his size. It wasn't completely ineffective, a fact that only irritated her further. He didn't scare her, and though she didn't think he intended to ignite the attraction she had never been able to shake, that was the result.

Ignite wasn't the right word...he'd fanned the flames already blazing inside her.

With slow, deliberate movements, she uncrossed her legs and stood, her gaze locked with his. He didn't give an inch, and her breasts brushed against his chest. Her nipples peaked with an aching need she couldn't suppress.

Thomas was the one man she'd never been able to ignore. Worse than that, a few days had left her with a persistent desire that seemed would last her entire lifetime. Five years ago, she had dismissed her feelings, chalking up the intensity to a small case of hero worship. He'd been legend in the dark ops community.

But that rationale had only carried her so far. It had been too late when she'd finally understood her feelings went beyond professional respect, far deeper than a mutual attraction sparked by convenient proximity and intense circumstances.

"Do you have any insight that will help me help you?"

His shuttered gaze drifted over her face, landing as effectively as a lover's sweet kiss on her lips. "With my case?"

Of course the case. "Yes," she managed to answer through a suddenly dry throat. She didn't want to hear his insights about her on a personal level.

"I don't think you misinterpreted anything. It's a very thorough report."

She counted it a professional victory and a personal loss when he stepped back. While her pulse resumed a rhythm closer to normal, she tried to keep her focus on business. So not an easy task.

"Just the allegations and launching the inquiry is bad enough for me." He rubbed a hand over the stubble shading his jaw. "Unless we find the bastard behind the plot, it's career-ending."

"Now you understand why I stepped up."

His expression was more confounded than comprehending, but he shrugged. "But why go to all this trouble to build a trap if the goal is to kill me?"

"Depends on the real end goal, I guess."

He picked up the tablet. "Or maybe two enemies are at odds about my future."

"I'm on your side, Thomas."

"And the committee?"

"I believe as a majority they want to be on your side. Can you say the same for Grant and Holt?"

"Without question," he replied.

She wasn't sure she agreed, since he said it without making eye contact, but to argue it without hard evidence wouldn't do any good. He was looking at the information again, combing through for the smallest kernel of intel that would give him a lead. She knew because she'd done the same thing.

He finally looked up again, setting the tablet aside. "In the morning, you should go back to D.C. I'll take it from here."

"No way." She shook her head; her gut instinct told her that would be a terrible mistake. "I didn't stick my neck out for you just to get a better view when they take you down."

"I'll land on my feet." His smile was full of regrets, an expression she'd never seen before. It worried her.

"Maybe. This time I think you need someone to break the fall."

"If you stay, it could mean the end of your career. Or worse, your life."

The part of her that had never gotten over their brief time together wanted to believe his concern was mostly personal, but Thomas was known for his concern for anyone he sent into the field. "I can take care of myself. You know you need someone watching your back on this."

He opened his mouth and she knew he was going to list all the times he'd managed just fine without her. Knowing it was true didn't mean she wanted to hear it.

She pressed her fingers gently to his lips. "Don't say it."
He frowned.

"It would be a waste of energy," she said. "You have a
partner this time. You'll just have to accept it."

His lips pursed and he kissed her fingers. She yanked
her hand back as if she'd been scalded. Before she could
step back, he caught her around the waist and pulled her
hard against his strong body.

So close, she could tally every new line bracketing his
eyes, framing his mouth. The mileage had done nothing
to lessen his appeal, it only strengthened her desire for
him. She watched the slow descent as he brought his lips
to meet hers, giving her the opportunity to duck or dodge.

Not a chance. She wanted this kiss—wanted *him*—more
than she wanted her next breath. He hesitated, his lips only
a whisper away and she leaned in, closing the gap. With
that first soft touch, the long, empty distance between their
last kiss and this one fell away. Once she'd thought time
and perspective would dull her desire; instead she discovered it had intensified her longing.

For him.

The sensual heat washed over her, sizzling through her
veins. She looped her arms around his neck, delighted and
meeting him with equal fervor as he took the kiss deeper.

"Jo, stop." His breath was ragged in her ear, his hands
firm on her hips as he nudged her away. "Stop."

"Why?" She blinked several times, slow to come out
of the sensual fog. "Oh." The "why" was clear in the hard
set of his jaw, the knitted brows. He may have given in
to the moment, but he clearly didn't want her the way she
wanted him.

Disappointment and humiliation whipped through her.
She took two quick steps back. The heat from the fire-

place behind her was weak compared to the burning passion he'd stirred in her blood. How could she have fallen so hard for this man?

An apology danced at the tip of her tongue, but she refused to let it out. She wasn't sorry, not really. If he gave her the slightest hint he wanted a repeat performance, she knew she'd leap at the chance.

Pathetic but true.

"Jo, I'm—"

"Don't say it." If he apologized, she might go screaming out into the storm. If he told her there was someone else, she'd feel lower than she already did. If that was possible. "Waste of energy," she quipped, managing a faint smile to go with it. "It's better if we keep this strictly business."

"That's—" Shoving his hands into his pockets, he gave a jerky nod. "Fine."

"We should make a list of people in your past, other than Whelan, who could have created that bomb." Grateful for the tablet in her hand, she turned on the screen. Instead of the file on Thomas's inquiry, she saw her files were open.

"You snooped through my files?" Outrage expelled the lingering heat he'd roused.

"Just in case I was wrong," he began, slumping back onto the couch.

"About trusting me," she finished for him.

"If it's any consolation, it isn't personal."

It wasn't. None of it. Not the snooping or the kiss. "I should be used to the derision and distrust by now." She was an idiot.

"You mean you aren't?"

"I guess a part of me is still naive enough to believe agents who work in the field should be used to oversight committees by now. Everyone has to answer to someone."

"Hindsight is twenty-twenty." He shrugged. "Knowing it doesn't mean liking it when someone with plenty of time and the whole story second-guesses decisions made in the line of duty."

"That's not what I do."

"Then you are an exception to the rule."

"I do my best. Please tell me who you think is responsible for the explosion and the setup."

"Whelan made that bomb, no doubt in my mind. His signature is in the scent on the fuse more than the design of a bomb. Whether he put it there or not is still a valid question, but if you say he's in the country, I believe he rigged it himself. As for the setup, I don't have enough information. That's why I checked your files. To see if there was more to this story than the report you showed me. Something you didn't see."

"Happy now?" she demanded, still frustrated.

He stood up to pace again. "I had to be sure."

"Got it." And on a professional level she understood. "You could have asked."

He chuckled, but the sound carried more bitterness than humor. "I know the training you've had. As head of a division I have a better idea what it takes to stay alive on the committee. I could ask if you had lunch on the moon and not be sure if your answer was truthful."

"We've received the same training, Thomas, and I trusted you despite the outbreak evidence and allegations you'd sold out."

She waited just long enough to see his face go pale as the full measure of her words sunk in. He couldn't do it, couldn't have that same faith in her. They were both tired and stressed out. Maybe he'd come around by morning. "With no connection to the outside world, there's nothing more we can do tonight. Get some rest. We can develop a plan to draw out Whelan and whoever is setting you up in the morning." She turned for the bedroom.

"Jo, wait."

Not a chance. She kept moving. She didn't trust herself to maintain the distance he obviously needed.

Chapter Ten

Glenstone Lodge, 10:00 p.m.

Lucas recognized the thinly veiled concern in Blue Drake's eyes as she and her husband approached his table. During his days as Thomas's deputy director of Mission Recovery, he'd served as her contact when she'd been assigned to protect Noah Drake, the man who'd not only married her, but eventually joined her as a Specialist.

The rest of the guests were divided between dancing, a card game and simply relaxing in good company.

"Good evening, Lucas. Can I have a minute?"

"Of course." He glanced across the table, making sure Victoria was distracted with her own conversation.

"There was an explosion in a long-term parking lot at the Denver airport a couple of hours ago," Blue said quietly. "It was on a breaking news update while I was in the lobby downstairs."

"As the storm was rolling in?"

"Yes, sir."

"Director Casey's flight landed safely. He called me."

"I'm glad to hear that," she said, visibly relieved. "He wouldn't have a car in long-term parking."

"No. I don't even think he intended to pick up his rental until tomorrow morning. He wasn't planning to drive in the storm." No matter that he knew this information, Lucas's instincts went on point.

"The authorities haven't released any names or picked up any suspects," Noah added.

Lucas was already mentally sifting through his contacts, wondering who he could call about video surveillance at the lot. He pulled out his cell phone, only to realize there was no signal. "Keep an eye on the news. If you hear anything that you think ties to Director Casey, let me know." They both nodded and Lucas turned the conversation in a lighter direction.

If Thomas had been in trouble when they spoke Lucas would have picked up on it. Had something gone wrong after their call ended?

A waiter moved to his side. "Mr. Camp, I'm sorry to disturb you, sir, but there's a message for you at the front desk."

Lucas excused himself and rose from the table. Moving slower than he would like and leaning heavily on his cane, he made his way out of the great room and to the lobby. His wife caught up with him just as he pushed the elevator call button.

"Is there a problem, Lucas?"

He shook his head. "Just a message waiting downstairs. Want to join me?"

"Always."

There were less than a handful of times he'd kept anything from her and he didn't see any need to add to that short list now. The elevator arrived and as the doors closed, he drew her into his arms. "Having a good time?"

"It's wonderful. Cecelia and Casey have outdone themselves with this one. Whoever in our growing family gets married next will have a tough time topping this."

"I worried the weather would upset her, but my god-daughter seems to find it romantic."

"Everything here is romantic," Victoria agreed. "As long as Thomas gets here safely for tomorrow's rehearsal it should stay that way."

Lucas smiled as the elevator chimed their arrival at the lobby level. "Nothing will keep him away. Has Casey expressed any concern?"

"Not yet."

He hoped the bride-to-be still felt the same way tomorrow because Lucas had a bad, bad feeling that something was very wrong.

"Mr. and Mrs. Camp," the woman behind the desk greeted them. "How are the festivities?"

"Absolutely marvelous," Victoria raved.

"That's what we like to hear." The clerk handed Lucas a folded note. "My apologies for the interruption, but we were told this needed to be delivered immediately, rather than placed in your mailbox."

Lucas accepted the note, thanked the woman and stepped aside to read it. Victoria waited patiently, but he felt her gaze on him, watching for his reaction. He read it repeatedly; it was only one brief line, but he wasn't quite sure what to make of the strange message. He only knew it meant trouble was hovering at the edges of the wedding, ready to strike.

He had suspected as much.

"Is it Thomas?" Victoria's hand on his arm accompanied her whisper.

"No, no. Thomas is fine." He hoped it wasn't a lie.

He stepped back up to the desk. "This came over the landline?"

"Yes, sir. Would you like me to check the caller ID?"

"Please." He showed Victoria the note while he tried to

formulate a reply. When the clerk reported the name of a motel just west of Denver, he asked them to return the call.

Lucas waited while the woman made the call and related his response, which consisted of no more than a time and his cell phone number; then he thanked her again.

Victoria was still pondering the strange message: *Whelan arrived four weeks ago ready to party. May attend with a date and a gift.*

"Sounds ominous. Should Cecelia adjust the seating chart?" she offered with a smile that held no amusement.

"That won't be necessary." Shaking his head, he pocketed the note as he guided her back to the elevator and the party. So many things in their line of work required privacy.

Until his last breath, he would strive to do everything in his power to protect Victoria from harm or distress. Not because she couldn't handle a crisis—she was beyond capable—but because she'd handled so many on her own through the years.

This time when the elevator doors closed, there was no embrace, just the flash of her eyes, so perceptive. "What should I know?"

"It would seem trouble is on the way." He leaned on his cane, debating the options.

"Do you know who this Whelan is?"

"Not personally." She sent him a questioning look. "He's known as an explosives expert and there was an incident this afternoon at the airport. It can't be a coincidence."

"What are you contemplating?"

"Not knowing who sent the message, it's hard to know just what I'm to do with the information."

"Why didn't you ask?" She handed him the note. "Is there a chance it was sent by this Whelan person himself?"

"No, this was sent from a Specialist."

Her gaze narrowed and he knew they were both wondering what business brought a Specialist to Denver, but not to the wedding. "Who?"

"We'll know soon enough."

She nodded thoughtfully. "You aren't going to sit back and wait."

He dropped a light kiss on her lips. "Would you? I'll talk to a few of the guests who can set up a watch and double-check the staff background. If this criminal is out to hurt Thomas or Casey or otherwise ruin her wedding day, he's in for a significant surprise."

"Hmm."

"What?"

"Any chance you'll let someone else head up the 'surprise'?" she asked as they exited the elevator.

"I suppose I have to." He feigned an innocent expression. "We're semi-retired."

Just as he'd hoped, she smiled as they walked back into the party.

Chapter Eleven

11:30 p.m.

Thomas tried to get comfortable on the couch in front of the fire, but he couldn't stop kicking himself. Being tired and frustrated didn't excuse how poorly he was coping with this situation. Personally or professionally.

Jo didn't deserve the brunt of his anger and frustration. None of the many rationalizations rolling through his brain would be enough to mend the rift he'd created. Only a sincere apology would work. Or the truth.

He wasn't ready to face that yet.

The truth was muddied up with his feelings, floating somewhere in the murky space between the past and the present. Johara DeRossi was special. Just thinking it, he recognized the words as an extreme understatement. He might have pushed her away for her own good way back then, but it felt like a monumental mistake now.

"Hindsight," he muttered, gathering the quilt Jo had been using. Looking back with the benefit of experience he might well have done things differently where she was concerned. Now it was too late. Wasn't it?

He distracted himself with speculation about the wedding party. Cecelia and Casey had booked the entire resort for several days. It had been a smart choice, considering the bride-to-be was CIA and the groom a Colby investigator. Their combined guest list meant security was as important as the dress or flowers for this wedding.

He knew tonight was just a casual reception. It was probably better he was stuck out here. Having logged his fair share of time in the field, he felt more comfortable navigating tricky terrain or elusive enemies than a ballroom full of friends and family. He certainly wouldn't have wanted Jo hovering at the fringes of the happy event in her official capacity, raising eyebrows or dragging his name through the mud on Casey's special day.

The lights flickered once, interrupting his thoughts, then the cabin went dark, except for the fire. Quiet fell almost as suddenly as the ambient noise from the refrigerator and furnace ceased to fill the air.

The second hand on the battery-operated wall clock shouted each passing second in the eerie stillness and he listened carefully for any creak or crunch of someone approaching outside. Instead there was only a shuffle followed by a thud from the bedroom. Sitting up, he softly called Jo's name.

"I'm fine," she replied.

The absolute silence that followed confirmed she, too, was listening for any sounds that didn't fit the weather conditions outside. Long minutes ticked by and the lack of footfalls, breaking glass or red dots from a laser sight had him breathing normally again.

Jo emerged from the hallway, pausing at the edge of the glow from the fire. "This is crazy," she muttered.

"Hard to believe the power lasted this long," he said, finally convinced it wasn't another attack.

"How could all weather radar miss something this big?"

He chuckled. "Did Mother Nature mess with your plans?"

"Yes," she said, her frustration evident. "It was supposed to be an easy thing. At least a civilized meet. We sit, we talk—"

"After I woke up from the sedative, you mean."

She snorted and shuffled closer. "I've explained that. Repeatedly. Build a bridge, Director, and get over it."

He smiled at the sight of the ever-elegant Agent DeRossi swaddled in a thick blanket shuffling closer to the fire. There wasn't a fireplace in the bedroom and she'd freeze back there without the furnace. "Is there a backup generator?"

She shrugged. "If there is, it would've been added by the management company and it wasn't mentioned in the rental brochure. Feel free to go look for one."

"I'll pass. Guess we're both better off out here tonight." He moved to put another log on the fire.

Her reply was an unintelligible grumble.

When the log caught, he shifted the couch and chair closer to the fire so they could rest more comfortably. He smiled, having never seen her disheveled. They'd come through a rather harrowing exit out of Germany and she'd never once let the stress show. She'd dug a bullet out of him and patched him up without being this shaken.

"The idea that I sold a weaponized virus really upsets you."

"No." She curled up in the chair, tucking her feet under her. "You being targeted by false accusations upsets me."

"Why?"

She was avoiding eye contact, another behavior he'd never witnessed before. He wanted to get to the root of her distress. For the case. *Right.* Quizzing her now was all about his own selfish curiosity.

"There is something bigger at play here, behind the scenes." She slid a glance his way. "Don't look at me like that. I haven't heard so much as a rumor. It's just a gut reaction. Maybe they were right about my inability to be objective where you're concerned."

As far as he knew this was the first time she'd been directly assigned to him or his Specialists. Her position gave her extensive access to most of the records and files anytime she wanted to exploit the advantage, but to his knowledge, the Initiative committee had never had cause to take an in-depth look at Mission Recovery.

Her announcement echoed in his brain a couple of times.

"What does that mean?"

She sighed and snuggled deeper into the chair, pulling the blanket snug up to her chin. "We're an oversight committee, Thomas. What do you think we do?"

"I thought you investigated when there was suspicious activity."

"There's a term that defines our general career paths."

"True. What prompted a closer look at Mission Recovery ops?"

"Your success."

"My team is suspect for being good at the job?"

"Yup."

"Initiative has never sanctioned us. Am I to believe that's because of you?"

"Who's fishing now?" She turned, finally looking him in the eye. "We both know your success is because you hire the best and they run clean ops."

"That must be devastating to the committee."

"More than you know."

"Be clear, Jo. Are you saying we should thank someone inside of Initiative for today's fun?"

"Maybe." She pushed a loose strand of hair behind her

ear. "It's just a working theory, but who else could claim there was a source without having to share it?"

"I can think of a few people in more than one agency."

"I know. And before you insist we risk life and limb to find another place for the night, let me reiterate there is no way anyone can trace this cabin to you or me."

"I wasn't going to insist on anything of the kind."

She shot him a doubtful glance.

"Not in this weather." And not since he'd made the call from the convenience store requesting an assist from Specialist Jason Grant. He wasn't sure what to think since she'd told him Grant was here in Denver, but he knew the man was loyal above all else. Jason would get the warning to Lucas at the lodge and if Whelan had something showy planned, Lucas would stop him.

"I owe you an apology. It seems we're safe enough, since no one's put us on the defensive."

"Thanks."

She was quiet for a while; he thought she might have dozed off, but weary as he was, Thomas couldn't sleep. He stared at the firewood stacked in the box, thought about the groceries in the kitchen. He couldn't help wondering how long Jo had been preparing for this weekend. All the signs pointed to a carefully staged and meticulously planned mission.

This little cabin wasn't something she'd rented on the fly because the Initiative told her to investigate him, no matter what she said. He understood, based on the intel she'd shared, why she was worried about his career. He believed that Middle Eastern village had been targeted and used to undermine his reputation and to cast doubt that would cause an all-out upheaval in Mission Recovery.

He wouldn't let that happen, but he understood the attempt and threat was real even though it was patently false.

It was the timing that niggled at him, forced him to look at Jo with as much, if not more, personal curiosity than professional distance.

The wedding date and destination had been set months ago. For the few people who knew him, it wasn't a stretch to know he'd clear his calendar and would attend the ceremony—Cecelia was the last of his family and her daughter was as close as he'd get to having a child of his own.

Someone obviously wanted him out of the way and chose the ideal time and place to attack. But why? Even if they caught up with Whelan, without a lead on the supposed buyer, he might never know who was behind this.

Jo shifted and he realized she was still awake. "How long have you been planning this ambush?" His voice sounded too loud in the quiet of the cabin and despite the bulk of the blanket wrapped around her, he saw her jump.

But when she turned to look at him her dark eyes were almost sad. "Haven't we been over this?"

He shrugged. "What else are we going to do?"

"Sleep? Make a plan for tomorrow?"

"We should sleep in shifts," he answered. "And my plan for tomorrow is to get up to Glenstone." He didn't have to add that he wouldn't go all the way to the lodge until they had this issue in hand. "How long, Jo?"

"I told you, the cabin is a rental."

"That doesn't really answer the question."

She tucked a wayward strand of hair behind her ear and her mouth twitched in a move he recognized as irritation. It was her one tell. Something she'd worked hard to overcome. If her self-control was slipping, it meant she was exhausted.

He felt a little guilty knowing he was going to exploit that weakness to get some real answers out of her.

"If we're sleeping in shifts, you take the first watch."

She closed her eyes and regulated her breathing, but she didn't fool him.

"So this is your mother's place?"

Her eyes flew open, all the pretense and masks of a trained field agent gone. "How could you know that?"

"You told me." It was a rare treat to see the woman behind the facade and he could count on one hand the number of times she'd been that open with him. "During that last night in Austria."

"I remember," she said with a tired sigh.

It wasn't quite the reaction he'd expected. He never allowed himself the luxury of regret, except where it pertained to her. As much as he tried to forget or ignore the shocking intimacy they'd shared on the Isely mission, he'd never been able to completely lock it away.

In the years since, he understood walking away from Johara DeRossi had been a necessity. Now he was thinking he'd done the wrong thing for all the right reasons.

"I only told you she had a place in the mountains. I never said which range. Her place might be in Nepal for all you know."

Her quiet voice brought him back to the present and carried him through the past simultaneously. They'd been lying together in a sumptuous bed, the first rays of dawn creeping around the edges of tasseled curtains. His palms tingled. Would her skin still feel like warm silk gliding under his hands? He tried to shake free of the memories.

"True, but in the current context it seems like the Rockies are the logical conclusion."

"Logic is one of your strengths." She pushed a hand through her hair again. "I swear to you, Thomas, no one in our line of work can trace this cabin to me."

"You're sure?"

He realized he didn't particularly care about the answer. They were alone, apparently safe enough, and both of them were too wired to rest. It seemed almost criminal to waste this opportunity to rekindle the blaze they'd once shared. A passion that might be all too ready to burn hot and fast again if that kiss was any indication. How many nights had he dreamed of her supple body nestled against his, her glossy black mane fanned across the pillows? He shifted, grateful the heavy quilt draped across his legs hid his reaction. Scaring her off wasn't what he had in mind.

"Keeping secrets and hidden agendas are my specialty," she said with a big yawn.

"Mine, too. But we both know how to dig up those secrets, too."

"I know."

No two words had ever sounded so loaded. "Feels like a tidy coincidence that this place just happened to be stocked and ready for visitors."

"There's a management company—didn't I mention that? They have a comprehensive staff. A staff who doesn't know who *I* am. When I need this place, I call and rent it like any other tourist."

"Of course. And they just happen to know my favorite brand of red sauce." It was, in fact, the only premade brand he used and only in emergencies. He supposed this qualified.

"Might have been the only brand on the shelf. More likely it was a lucky guess."

"It's far too late to play dumb, Jo. Dodging a couple of tactical assaults doesn't mean we're out of the woods."

"Pun intended?"

"If it fits," he said, grinning at her.

"Oh, put that away." She flicked a hand at his face.

"What?"

"There. The frown is much better."

"You're not making sense."

"Now who's playing dumb? You know what that charming little smirk does to me. *Did* to me," she amended.

He didn't know he had a charming smirk and he couldn't imagine charm having any effect on Jo in either a public or private setting. She always followed her own agenda with determination and focus. The idea of being able to charm her was interesting and something he might enjoy digging into in more detail. When he wasn't sorting out who was trying to kill him.

"When and why did you book this little getaway?"

He'd almost decided she didn't plan to answer as several more minutes passed with only the sound of her soft breathing and the occasional snap and crackle of the fire.

"About four months ago I called and booked the cabin for several days before and after the wedding."

The wedding had been planned long before that. Casey and her mother knew he'd be in attendance from the moment his niece announced her engagement. Anyone who knew him would know that.

"As the date grew closer, I grew more convinced that I needed a face-to-face with you. So I made the final arrangements. Borrowed a few of your clothes and mailed the RSVP card still lying on your kitchen counter."

At his pointed look, she added, "I wanted to cover all the bases. I'm your plus one, just in case I needed to crash the wedding."

For her to take that kind of risk, letting herself into his house, there had to be more to this story. He hadn't bothered with the RSVP card since his niece and sister knew he was coming. "What happened exactly to prompt all these advance preparations?"

"Nothing in particular," she said, turning to face him once more. "That was the problem. Certain things weren't adding up and it was like an itch between my shoulder blades. I couldn't pin it down no matter which angle I took. My plan was to catch up with you on your way to or from the wedding and get your opinion."

"The committee wouldn't have endorsed that."

She rolled her eyes. "Which is why I wanted to meet somewhere other than a secure conference room."

And yet this was the first she'd mentioned her doubts about her own department. "Then the outbreak changed your mind about me?"

"Don't be absurd. You're no more capable of betraying this country than I am. It just changed the timeline."

He thought about the evidence she'd shown him, and more specifically about the copy of an email in her file that someone had forwarded to her about the outbreak. "Have you traced the email back to the source?"

"No. Which is part of my problem. We might take a closer look at something based solely on a vague informant, but we've never launched a full investigation without some sort of corroborating evidence. And the investigator typically has full access and authority."

Considering where they were and how they'd gotten here, it felt like she had the authority aspect firmly under control.

"What did they give you the authority to do with me?"

Her laughter was as brittle as the air outside. "The most I can do is arrest you. Any idea that I would take a more permanent action against you is simply being melodramatic or paranoid."

Stunned, Thomas gaped at her. Drama wasn't something he or anyone on his team indulged in. Paranoia, on the other hand, wasn't as bad as she made it sound.

"Let's go back a few months," he said. "The supply audits. Do you think someone was looking for the virus?"

"I only knew about one audit, but in light of everything between then and now, I'd say it's likely."

"I wouldn't store anything incriminating at Mission Recovery. Not if I intended to sell it off."

"Which is why I searched your house."

He was sure he'd misunderstood her. "Care to repeat that?"

Exasperated, she rolled her eyes. "Would you have preferred someone else go through your things?"

He could rail about legalities, but the truth was in their line of work, that line was often blurred in the quest for immediate justice. Technically, his career and his entire team of Specialists didn't legally exist. While he often exploited that to the benefit of the mission it was a double-edged sword that sliced against him now.

"How do we get in front of this?"

"I don't know," she admitted. "Honestly, I thought I was in front of it when I met you at the airport. Obviously I wasn't there alone."

"Did you see someone other than Jason?"

Her mouth twitched again and she was suddenly absorbed by the pattern in the quilt.

Thinking back to her face when she met him at the rental car line he said, "Let me rephrase. Who *else* did you see at the airport?"

"Only Grant." She peered up, and he knew she was trying to read his reaction. "I thought maybe there was someone else, but it was only him. At first I thought maybe he was here for the wedding, but he tailed me for days before you arrived."

"So he knew about the rental car—"

"Cars," she clarified.

"And the cabin, too?"

"No. He knows about a hotel suite I booked for us."

"Us?" To his dismay, memories of the hotel suite in Austria filled his mind. Where was his objectivity? His career, even his life, depended on figuring this out. It was hardly the time for his more basic urges to dominate his thinking.

"I told you he didn't rig that bomb or even push the trigger," Thomas said, scrubbing at the stubble on his chin.

"Who are you trying to convince?"

"I don't need to convince anyone. I know my agents." Pieces of his well-ordered world were all too ready to fracture and splinter. He knew Jason was clean. In this business gut instinct counted for so much. When he'd had the chance at the convenience store to call any number of people for help, he had called Jason.

"So you knew he was assigned to tail me."

He shook his head, refusing to lie to her, even though it made him look bad. "No."

"Then Holt must have sent him out. Unless your agents have the authority to go off on their own assignments."

"If that were true—" and he wasn't about to admit she wasn't far off the mark "—why would Grant follow you? Most likely Holt caught wind of your investigation."

She yawned and he automatically mimicked her. The events of the day were catching up to both of them. She might have been ready to intercept him, but the explosion and chase had been a shock to her.

It sure as hell had been a shock to him.

"That's what I thought, too, when I first spotted Grant. Your team is so dedicated to you." Her eyelids were drooping. "I had fun leading him around on a couple of shopping sprees."

"Really?"

"Yeah." She gave him a sleepy grin. "I visited some exclusive girl-power boutiques."

"What'd you buy?" His imagination was filling in blanks that he had no business thinking about. Shoes. Maybe those heels she'd worn today were new. Did she have a weakness for shoes? "Jo?"

This time she really was asleep. "Guess I've got first watch," he whispered. It didn't bother him as he knew he wouldn't be able to sleep with so much on his mind and her so close. Still, he seemed content just to take in the view of her beautiful face while she wouldn't know he was watching. Her features were exotic and slender, dark and alluring. She had mesmerized him the first time he'd laid eyes on her. And if that weren't enough she was endlessly fascinating. Intelligent and determined.

One of her bare feet peeked out from the blanket. He got up and adjusted the blanket to cover it, then changed his mind. Gently scooping her into his arms, he shifted her to the couch, where she could be more comfortable. The feel of her soft, small body almost undid him. He wanted her with a ferocity that caught him off guard.

Somehow he had to protect her from whatever the hell this was.

With nothing else to do but listen to the fire and watch the snow pile higher, he settled into the chair and deconstructed everything he'd learned from her preliminary file and current events.

Sometimes it was impossible to nail down trouble unless you went backward...beyond the beginning and retraced the steps required to get to a certain place.

He watched the sleeping woman who had haunted his dreams for five years.

If they survived, he needed to retrace their steps...to that place that only this woman had ever taken him.

Chapter Twelve

With a kiss, Lucas left Victoria with tea in their suite and went down to the dining room for breakfast. She preferred her quiet time in the mornings.

Some days he couldn't believe he was lucky enough to be with her. Maybe it was being surrounded by the happiness of the bride and groom and an entire resort full of contented people, but he couldn't stop smiling. After all the years of dedication and sacrifice for the job, being here right now with Victoria and so many friends made it all worthwhile.

The resort had a full breakfast buffet going and he smiled to himself as agents he'd known through both the Colby Agency and his own time with Mission Recovery came and went, alone or with families in tow.

Outside the big bank of windows, the mountains glistened with more than a foot of fresh snow. Most of the children and several adults were chatting about what snowy adventure to tackle first.

He walked down to the front desk and asked for the manager.

"Good morning, Mr. Camp." The lady flashed a bright smile.

"Good morning." Lucas was quite impressed with the service here. "Have you heard anything about the condition of the roads in Denver? More specifically between Denver and Glenstone? Our final guest was delayed by yesterday's storm."

He'd expected Thomas to call first thing this morning, but so far, he hadn't heard a word. The cell towers were back up and working now. If the roads were clear he should be on his way. As excited as he knew Thomas was about this, and after the cryptic message, he'd been looking forward to that phone call. It seemed they had much to discuss.

"Denver got buried in fifteen inches," she explained. "A storm this early plays havoc with plows but the thoroughfares should be clear by midday at the latest."

"Do you think it will take a ski lift to get him up here?"

The manager gave a nod. "If he shows up in Glenstone and his car can't handle the climb up to us, we'll send a driver or even a snowmobile. Everyone who was on the schedule this morning had no trouble with the roads, but they're locals and used to winter driving."

"Good." Lucas was pleased the manager had inadvertently given him another important detail: everyone who was supposed to be at the lodge was here. "He's giving the bride away and I have a feeling she's not going down that aisle without him."

"Whatever it takes to make her day all she's dreamed it would be, that's what we'll do."

"Thank you."

Lucas pulled out his cell phone and put a call through to Thomas's cell number one more time as he moved on to the dining room and the scents of breakfast. Once more, the call went immediately to voice mail. Having left two messages already, he didn't bother to leave a third.

Spotting Blue at the coffee service table, he joined her. They exchanged a quick greeting before she got straight to the point. "Have you heard from the director?"

"Not so far." He pocketed the phone and produced a smile. "I was just trying to get through. Any update on the explosion?" He'd purposely left the television off in hopes that Victoria wouldn't hear anything more disturbing than what she suspected already.

Thomas Casey might very well be in trouble.

Blue stirred cream into her coffee. "Nothing other than one car obliterated and several others with varying degrees of damage. If they have leads, they aren't saying so."

Lucas debated making another call to local law enforcement and decided against it.

"Maybe he overslept," Blue said. "The altitude can do that."

He gave her a skeptical look. They were talking about Thomas Casey here.

"Fair enough." She relented with a nod. "Oversleeping isn't something Director Casey would do. Is there anything you need from Noah or me? I've alerted my colleagues. Whatever trouble might be brewing, we're braced for it."

He patted her shoulder. She was one of his favorite people, brave and dedicated to both her career and her husband. "For now, just enjoy yourself. I'm sure there's a simple explanation for his delay. But being prepared is an excellent idea."

It was Blue's turn to give him a look loaded with skepticism. "But you're worried."

He smiled. "At the moment my biggest concern is upsetting Casey. I want this entire weekend to be one she will treasure for the rest of her life."

"We'll help keep her distracted. I'm sure he'll be here in time for the rehearsal. Several of us are planning to take advantage of the fresh snow. Though no one is skiing until after the ceremony. Don't want any injuries getting in the way of the festivities. Want to join in?"

It sounded like just the kind of fun they could all use but he needed to stay on top of this situation with Thomas. Lucas spotted his wife at the doorway. He excused himself and pushed his concerns for Thomas aside and walked over to greet her.

"I thought you were enjoying some quiet time," he said.

"I was going to surprise you with fruit and cream. The strawberries look delicious."

She looped her arm through his. "The room was just too lonely without you."

Lucas brushed a kiss across her cheek. He was indeed a lucky man.

When they were seated, with a pot of coffee and a plate of fruit between them, he filled her in on some of the plans to enjoy the snow.

"I'd love to join in, but I'll settle for supervising the snowmen building. Jamie and Luke will be in the middle of it and you know I can't resist anything when it comes to our grandchildren."

"Afraid you'll lose the war-of-the-sexes snowball fight?"

She searched his face for a moment. "Why don't you tell me what's really on your mind this morning, Lucas?"

He paused, the coffee mug halfway to his lips. Carefully he returned it to the table. "What are you implying, my dear?"

"You haven't heard from Thomas."

He wasn't sure how she did that and some days he wished she didn't possess such perceptive powers. It would make for protecting her far easier. "He's not answering his cell."

"Maybe he's with his plus one."

"I beg your pardon?" Thomas would have told him if he'd planned to bring a guest to the wedding.

"I was chatting with the bride and her mother last night. Thomas returned the RSVP card with a 'plus one.'" She put it in air quotes as if that would help him make sense of it.

"And you're just now telling me?" That was certainly an interesting development. Thomas Casey had enjoyed his share of romantic interludes, Lucas felt confident, but he never indulged in a personal relationship. He was too focused on the job. Lucas had warned him that he was going to wake up alone one morning and wish he'd taken the time to have a home life.

"You've been distracted," Victoria pointed out.

"He must have been making room on the guest list for a new Specialist." Which begged the question: Why would the director of Mission Recovery feel the need to do that?

Victoria shook her head, a small pitying smile on her lips. "I doubt it."

"Well, I know he's not dating anyone. Thomas Casey doesn't date."

"Are you sure?" Her smug grin faded. "I hoped to get all the details out of you."

"The high altitude and all these happy wedding vibes have skewed your thinking," he teased.

"Oh, I resent that." She chose a slice of melon and ignored him for a moment. "Levi and Casey are so in love, it is easy to see hearts and flowers everywhere," she finally allowed. "That doesn't change his RSVP card."

"Those had to be turned in two or three weeks ago."

"His continued absence is beginning to make you wonder if something is awry at Mission Recovery."

He nodded. "I'm afraid so."

"I could blame your concerns on a lack of oxygen, too. Paranoia is known to be a symptom."

"Only extreme cases," Lucas said with a wry smile. He topped off his coffee, his mind flipping through the various scenarios that could delay Thomas. They both knew neither paranoia nor altitude had his instincts prickling like this.

"Cecelia says he cleared his calendar for this weekend."

"That's what worries me most." Cecelia was Thomas's sister and the mother of the bride.

"You know him best, but I don't believe he would willingly combine any sort of business with Casey's wedding unless he had no other choice."

"You're absolute correct, my dear, not willingly," he said with a meaningful look. "But the man has enemies who would gladly take a shot at him if the opportunity arose."

His wife laid her hand over his. "Unfortunately, we all do, Lucas."

"I know." He drummed up a smile, to forget the more dire scenarios nagging at him.

"But you want to do something."

"He hasn't called. Considering the explosion last night, and the tip about Whelan, he would have called if he was in the position to. But there isn't even a message."

"So call Holt. I'll go to the buffet and give you some privacy."

Lucas stood as his wife left the table, then resumed his seat and pulled up the number on his cell phone. He'd been in Holt's shoes, serving as Deputy Director to Thomas Casey. It wasn't an easy job and in Holt's shoes, he wouldn't appreciate a surprise inquiry from a predecessor. Yet, under the circumstances, it was the logical move. Holt, provided he had the right information, could quickly put Lucas's worries to rest.

He waited through three frustrating rings for an answer. "Good morning, Lucas."

Lucas wasn't surprised by the informal greeting; Mission Recovery had all the tech toys and, being retired, Lucas didn't try to hide his trail so much anymore.

"Have you heard from Director Casey this morning?"

"I thought he was with you."

"An early blizzard hit Denver yesterday. He agreed to wait it out in the city."

Hearing Holt's note of surprise, Lucas made a conscious effort not to read too much into the sound.

"I assumed he made it to the lodge and couldn't call because the networks were down," Holt said at last.

"When was he supposed to check in?" Cleared schedule or not, Lucas knew his friend. Thomas would want to be kept up to date while he was out of the office.

Again, Holt hesitated, but this time Lucas understood it was about security protocols. "You know my clearance is still valid," he growled into the phone.

"That isn't the issue, Lucas. He missed last night's call and I'd hoped he missed this morning's check-in because he was distracted with the wedding."

But Lucas and Holt both knew there was zero chance of the director missing two check-in calls unless he was physically incapacitated. Thinking of Whelan, he didn't want to discuss it on an open line in a busy dining room. "Are there any open cases?"

"Always."

"In this area," Lucas clarified.

"Of course not."

Lucas interpreted that too-quick reply as a yes. "Well, that's something. The bride needs him. Call me when you hear something. I'll do the same. At what point are you engaging a team?"

"A wedding doesn't warrant a recovery op," Holt snapped.

His flare of temper seemed unwarranted in Lucas's

opinion. "No. But a missing director sure as hell does. I can put an asset on the task if I need to. I have the personnel right here."

"Is that a threat?"

Lucas hoped that was the man's insecurities showing and nothing more. "Not a threat, Holt. It's a promise."

"They aren't your personnel anymore, Camp. You have no authority."

So this was the way it was going to be. "You're right, of course." Lucas smiled as his wife returned to the table. "They're Casey's personnel."

Holt swore. "If he doesn't call by noon, I'll send someone out."

That was more like it. "Thank you. Always a pleasure." He ended the call and slid the phone into his pocket.

Victoria's eyebrows arched. "Progress?"

"Holt says Thomas didn't check in last night or this morning. If neither of us hears anything by noon, Holt will put a Specialist on his trail."

"Good." She took his hand in hers. "Why are you still frowning?"

Lucas leaned close to her ear, giving the impression he was whispering something personal to his beloved wife. "Holt was reluctant to send anyone."

"I see." She kissed him lightly on the cheek. "Let's finish our breakfast first," she whispered back. "Then we'll talk it through."

Just when he thought he couldn't love her more, he felt those ties growing even stronger.

Chapter Thirteen

Johara woke to the savory scent of bacon wafting through the air. Stretching under the warm quilt, she indulged in the momentary fantasy that this was just a relaxing weekend away from the politics and dangers of the real world.

Sunlight streamed through the windows and the view of the snow-covered trees sparkled like diamonds. Her stomach rumbled, interrupting the peaceful moment, and a deep chuckle echoed behind her.

She dragged her gaze from the window to take in the even better view of Thomas holding out a mug of steaming coffee.

"Thought you could use the boost."

"Thanks." She sipped carefully and then wrapped both hands around the thick ceramic mug. "Good morning."

"Definitely," he answered, though she hadn't posed it as a question. "Breakfast is almost ready."

She set the mug aside as she got to her feet and folded the quilt. "Do I have time for a shower?"

"If you're quick about it."

She darted down the hallway to the bathroom and rushed through an abbreviated version of her morning routine, trying to figure out why he was so chipper.

He was a morning person, a fact she overlooked as a

side effect of his career. She, as he'd clearly recalled, pre-ferred caffeine to dull the sharp edge of early hours.

In fresh clothes, her damp hair pulled back in a sleek ponytail, she joined him in the kitchen. He was thought-ful enough not to ask her questions or chatter at her until the caffeine had a chance to kick in. Savoring the bacon and eggs, she felt almost human by the end of her second cup of coffee.

"No one has ever fixed breakfast for me," she said as she cleared the dishes.

"No one?"

"Not since I left home." She washed the dishes and set them in the dish drainer, refusing to let him dry this time. "Aside from the improved weather, why are you so happy this morning?"

"We haven't been found."

She topped off her coffee, did the same for him. "Fair point."

"You could smile about it."

"I could." She raised her mug to her lips to hide that she wanted to do just that. "Are we reconnected to the world yet?"

"Yes." He tapped the edge of the tablet sitting right where she'd left it last night.

He looked so pleased with himself it worried her. "You checked up on me."

"Well, yes. It's habit. But I also found a lead."

That news brought her back to the table in a hurry. "How?"

"One of the bullets hit the luggage rack. I dug it out and took a couple of pictures with your tablet."

The man had been up for a while and quite busy, it seemed. Her stomach clenched and she thought breakfast might make an unwelcome return appearance. "What did you do?" She set the coffee aside.

He frowned at her. "Nothing that would jeopardize our safety." He turned the tablet so she could see the enlarged picture of the bullet on the screen. "There were no prints, but I'd bet my life that this bullet will match at least one other bullet in the system."

She glanced up. "Are you telling me you've memorized a striation pattern?"

"Even if I had, it would never stand up as real evidence." He held up a small disposable container and slid it across the table. "The bullet. Open it, and take a look for yourself."

She sank into the chair and popped open the container. A plain look wasn't hard evidence, but she dutifully studied the .38 slug, comparing it to the picture on the tablet. "You've taken a fine picture, Director."

"Don't patronize me, Jo. That particular picture is from a different case."

She swiped the screen and barely stifled an oath. "You accessed the database with my login?" Tension turned to panic at the thought of either of their departments finding them before she could clear his name.

"No. And before you explain why that sends you into a panic, I'll tell you I downloaded that photo from my personal archive that I keep on a cloud server."

The swell of panic drained away. "Good," she whispered.

"Why?" He leaned across the table, his hand warm over hers. "You've expressed concerns about your office. What's really going on?"

She shook her head and pressed her lips together. "In a minute," she managed to say. "Tell me more about the bullets."

"You know as well as I do that only a small percentage of criminals in the world bother to make their own ammunition. This particular .38 ammunition has a powder blend as special as the designer. Smell it."

She held the open container to her nose and caught a scent like burnt oranges.

"This bullet is made by the same man who prefers big, showy displays of destruction like we saw yesterday."

"Whelan was shooting at us?"

"Yes. Well, at least his ammunition was. The scent doesn't last long obviously, so without the gun, we'll never tie these bullets together or wrap up the related cases."

"When did you tick him off?"

Thomas leaned back and laughed, with more than a little pride mixed in. "Germany was a productive trip."

"When?"

"You know when." His smile faded and his gaze slid away from hers. "Five years ago. I cost him a lot of money when I took down the Isely family."

Jo paced away from the table. "Did he ever have access to the virus?"

"Not that I know of."

"It just feels like this elaborate setup is a bit out of his league. From the little I've heard about him, he's a loner."

"He is, but he has plenty of connections around the world and I have plenty of enemies who might have hired him."

She knew that was true, it had been one more reason to take the investigation. Picking up the tablet, she took a closer look at the bullet. "Tell me more." Maybe it would help her put the scattered pieces in order.

"Whelan adds that distinct orange fragrance to his explosives. I caught the scent just before the rental car blew up. He likes his victims to know who did them in."

"A signature like that is easy to imitate." He arched an eyebrow, clearly annoyed, and she held up her hands. "Hey, I'm just playing devil's advocate here."

"You know I looked through your files, Jo." He dipped his chin at the tablet. "I saw the report that he entered the country with an unnamed U.S. escort."

"I wasn't the one who let him in," she said. "I didn't even know until long after it was done."

"But you know who was there and why they're working with him."

"No. I really don't know who it was or even which agency. I've told you everything, shared everything that's available to me. They cooperated with Whelan because he claims he can identify your next buyer."

"There is no buyer." Getting to his feet, Thomas snatched the container back and covered it. "I don't even have the virus."

"But someone does." She stared down at the tablet, her hands cold as she read a new email message. "I've been told the sale is set for two o'clock Saturday afternoon in Glenstone." The small village at the base of the mountain below the lodge where Casey Manning was to get married. This was not good for so very many reasons.

"What?" He didn't shout, but she winced anyway. "There's no way I'd do that. I haven't done that." He swore, using a few choice words that were new even to her.

"Read it for yourself," she said, turning the tablet toward him. "I have to say, looking at the way you operate this is exactly what someone who had studied your file would believe you'd do. Whoever this is, he knows you, Thomas."

He looked up from the email, jaw slack. "How can you say that? I'd never jeopardize family."

"It's not me saying it," she said gently. "It's a third party looking to set you up. This is very specific, Thomas."

"Too specific. Whelan's a piece of work, but I can't believe he'd be able to hack agency email systems or put all these accusations in place."

"With a U.S. agency vouching for him, an inside job is the only logical conclusion." She watched Thomas pace the length of the cabin as he wrestled with the implications. It was obvious he wanted to deny the betrayal of someone within Mission Recovery—and he might very well be right. But someone was using a vengeful and motivated bomber to take him out. Someone who knew his methods, likely based on previous missions.

"Please sit down."

He slumped into a chair. "It has to be CIA. Someone he bargained with to avoid prosecution for another crime. Has to be," he muttered.

"How would Whelan know about the wedding location?"

"An agent fed him the information and then trickled it to you. Hell, the agent might even have caused the outbreak to increase the urgency to reel me in." Thomas's blue eyes blazed with fury. "I'm here to give the bride away. That's all. I doubt I would have had time to leave the resort with all the things Casey and my sister had planned. Even if I had the damned virus, I wouldn't sell it. And if the CIA wants my buyer—I assume that's the bill of goods they sold the committee—"

She nodded.

"Why let him kill me?"

"He slipped the leash? Maybe they don't know Whelan's lying about you, the virus and the buyer. If this was his gig from the beginning maybe that's his end game."

Thomas grunted and pushed a hand through his short

hair. "That's the only plausible part of this whole situation. Whelan has every reason to want me dead." He stalked over to the window, turning the container over and over in his hands.

"Thomas." When he didn't reply, she got up and went to him. "Thomas, I came here to protect you. You have to believe that."

"I do." But the grief in his eyes when he looked at her ripped open a heart she'd never managed to keep closed against him.

She could no more deny him than stop her heart from beating. "I'd planned to discuss everything in a quiet, civilized manner *after* the wedding." And hopefully laugh about the ridiculous nature of the accusation. If everything had gone smoothly on a professional level, she'd intended to seduce him, hopefully reclaiming some of the magic they'd shared five years ago. "Then word came down that you were making 'another sale' possibly at the wedding itself." She put the phrase in air quotes to emphasize her low opinion of the rumor. "I was told to observe, but not intervene with the exchange."

"Nothing ominous about that," he grumbled sarcastically.

"Exactly my thought," she said. "In light of that development, it seemed best to intercept you before you reached Glenstone."

"Mission accomplished."

"Thanks. Tell me why Whelan's so intent on harming you that he'd lie to the CIA in order to get his shot at you and we can figure this out. Together. It has to be about more than money."

He was silent for so long, she knew he was turning over the options. She moved to the window and looked outside, wondering what miracle a snowplow could muster against the thick layer of white blanketing the landscape. Deep snow hid the SUV's tires and part of the front bumper. But the car's roof was swept clear from Thomas's early morning examination. The path Thomas had created when he'd checked the car and found the bullet looked like a narrow canyon. He'd never forgive her if he missed the wedding. For that matter, when Casey and Cecilia found out Jo was the problem, she was likely to find her name on an unofficial CIA hit list.

"We should try and clear the car," she said just to break the unbearable silence. Apparently there were things he didn't want her to know…still.

"It can wait a few more minutes." He came up behind her. "Does the committee know you intercepted me already?"

"If they do, they didn't hear it from me. And they won't."

"Meaning?"

"We have carte blanche in our investigations. As long as I have the report in on time, no one tells me how to do my job."

"So they didn't know *how* you intended to tail me."

"Correct."

"Which means they don't know which of your aliases or disguises to look for and yet they found us at the airport parking lot."

She pointed a finger at him. "They're looking for *you*. And for whoever Whelan says is the buyer." Boy, he'd taken her off the track of why Whelan wanted him so badly.

"What if we get to Glenstone and Whelan says you're the buyer?"

That suggestion landed as effectively as a punch in the gut. She didn't protest, because it could very well be true. "If so, why tell me the location of the meeting?"

"Because he won't give up his quest or the perks involved until tomorrow at two o'clock. He can say whatever he wants in the meantime, point to anyone at the time of the meet. We both know the buyer is just a fairy tale."

He was right. "It's not looking much like a happy ending is in store for either one of us."

He gazed at her with such intensity it stole her breath. "I gave up on my happy ending years ago," he confessed.

How many years ago? Her entire being from her heart to the depths of her soul longed to ask the question. But she just couldn't do it. She rubbed her arms and yanked the conversation back to business.

"Thomas, how do you want to proceed?"

"Do I have enemies on the Initiative committee?"

"Everyone does," she replied candidly. "But to answer your real question, no, I don't believe this witch hunt started at my office. We're being fed some clever and damaging details from an anonymous source. Your CIA theory fits."

She could practically see the gears turning as he reviewed all she'd said.

"Why are you being so honest with me?"

"You've never given me a reason to lie to you."

He seemed to add that to the rest of the processing going on inside his head.

"So your superiors don't know your intention is to help me beat these bogus charges."

"Nope. They only know the files I pulled while I was still at the office as I prepared my investigation. How I proceed in the field is my business."

"Nice gig."

"Your own Specialists have it much the same, don't they?"

"Not exactly." He pushed his hands into his pockets and

rocked back on his heels. It was a move he made when he'd reached a conclusion.

She wondered when he'd tell her about it, wondered if she'd like it. "Now who's fibbing?" She smiled as she shook her head. "You know autonomy can be dangerous. My boss isn't obligated to tell me the sources that lead to my investigations. It's my job to go out and try to confirm or deny various infractions or problems."

"Problems like me, a director turned traitor."

She held up her hands in surrender. "A director with a great deal of autonomy of his own."

"Not as much as you think. My system has checks and balances. I have to check in." He nodded toward the cuckoo clock on the wall. "In fact I've missed two calls already and with my phone in the ashes of that fire…"

"Your deputy director will send out a Specialist to rescue you."

"A man can hope," he said with a wink.

Oh, he'd made a decision all right, and she was growing more certain she wasn't going to like it. "What are you plotting, Director Cascy?"

"For right this minute?"

"Yes."

"A snowball fight seems the best option."

"I beg your pardon?"

He jerked a thumb over his shoulder toward the window. "In case you weren't sure, we're stuck here for at least a day. Unless you know who to call for a snowplow."

"If we can't get out, we're vulnerable."

He frowned again. "You said no one knew about this place."

"No one does," she said, the tension across her shoulders easing a fraction. Only a fraction. "Unless they managed to pick up our trail after all."

"Under a foot of snow? That's unlikely."

"But what about the euro? I disabled the rental company's GPS but—"

"I was under the car last night and saw no sign of a tag. If they had tagged the rental, I'm sure they would have made an appearance the minute the storm cleared. From what you've said, the person pulling the strings still expects me to show up in Glenstone or at the lodge. We're well south and east of both when there are other places we might have stopped on the direct route."

She hoped he was right and that was enough to protect them. "But if we can't get out today, you'll miss the rehearsal dinner."

His scowl deepened. "I'm aware of that, too. When I landed in Denver I joked with Lucas that I should find skis. Now I wish I had."

"Snowmobiles would be better," she muttered. This wasn't going at all as she'd planned. If not for spotting Jason Grant at the airport she might have stuck with her first idea and intercepted after the wedding and the supposed sale of the virus.

Suddenly the cabin didn't feel safe at all. Jason Grant had been top of his class as a sniper and served in both the military and local law enforcement. If he knew they were here, that she "stole" his director, or worse, if he was working with those trying to discredit Thomas…

"The management agency knows there's a renter up here this weekend," she considered aloud. "I'm sure they'll send someone to clear the road. We'll get you to the resort in time to walk Casey down the aisle. Hopefully tonight, but definitely by tomorrow."

"First things first," he said stepping close enough to crowd her.

She cursed her skittering pulse, but she held her ground. Barely. He couldn't possibly be entertaining the same romantic fantasy she'd been struggling to ignore since they arrived safely last night.

This was Thomas Casey, famous for his ability to escape impossible missions and terrible danger unscathed. His focus and dedication to the task were legendary and, providing she kept her hormones in check, they'd rescue his reputation before it suffered permanent damage.

"We have to neutralize whoever set this in motion," he was saying. "I won't lead an explosives expert to the wedding and put Casey and the rest in danger."

"What do you suggest?"

"I want to pick apart the Germany mission while we wait for the snowplow. It's the only place we worked closely. The only place the virus and Whelan intersect."

"Okay." She'd only been the contact and egress for the Isely case. She hadn't known anything about Whelan. She wasn't sure how much help she could offer him, but she'd damned give him her best effort.

"Assuming the snowplow arrives soon, let's make a reservation in Glenstone for tonight and tomorrow."

Startled, it took her a second to react. "In which name?" They both had more than one alias they could use long enough to get a hotel reservation. Grateful for the excuse, she stepped away from the heat his presence stirred to retrieve the tablet and open a search.

"Use my real name."

She pressed her fingers to her eyes. "You want to bait Whelan."

"I want to bait the person who hired him."

"It's a mistake."

"Why?"

THOMAS WATCHED HER chew on her full lower lip a moment. It was a temptation and a distraction he couldn't afford, but he was helpless to look anywhere else. They needed to leave before he said to hell with his reputation and the wedding and he just gave in to the weather and circumstances for a chance to be alone with her.

Never before had he entertained the idea of forgetting the job and the various crises plaguing the real world. But that's what Jo did to him. He told himself he'd walked away five years ago to protect her, that his work put anyone he cared about at risk. If he didn't get them out of here soon, the truth would be inescapable.

She made him want something he gave up long ago. Intimacy. Companionship. Something that went deeper than a fast affair between two agents killing time or playing a role on the job. He longed to hold her for hours, to stay hidden away and out of reach of spies, lies and covert operations. Johara DeRossi represented too many things he couldn't have.

"Wouldn't the great Thomas Casey have more sense than to use his real name when brokering a deal like this?"

"I'd think anyone who thinks I'd betray my country at my niece's wedding is banking on me to be just that arrogant."

She tilted her head as she weighed his suggestion. "You have a point."

He knew that. Still it stung she agreed so readily. Was this insecurity now? Good grief, how much lower would he fall before this wedding party turned nightmare was over?

"Come here and help me choose a place."

"You don't need my input."

"If you don't I'll use your card to book the most expensive option."

"You've done that before."

"I have indeed." Her dark eyes danced with mischief under those thick lashes. Was she thinking about the last hotel room they'd shared? God help him, he'd never managed to erase the memories. Even now, he struggled to chase the images from his mind.

"Then go for it. I assume in this fairy tale I'm getting paid handsomely for the virus, I might as well enjoy the money."

"Want to give me some tactical data to work with?"

"No need. Book anything. We aren't actually going there tonight, we just want Whelan and whoever he's working with to think we are."

"All right." She had the reservation made and confirmed in less than two minutes. "Consider it done."

"Jo." His throat dry, he swallowed and tried again. He had to focus on the business. "Can you pull up a map of Glenstone?"

"Mmm-hmm."

He walked up behind her, careful to keep enough distance since a touch would be awkward. Thomas took one look at the bird's-eye view of the mountain village and knew his plan could work. The small business district was split by one main street, several blocks long. The mountains crowded one side, a valley fell away on the other. Yes, whoever was playing him knew all about the Germany mission. It narrowed the list of enemies considerably. Down to one, actually.

Whelan, with cleverly orchestrated help, was here to take him out. At least it made the motive clear enough. The man was all about the money and Thomas had cost him plenty when he'd taken down the Isely family. But there was more. He had made Whelan look bad.

He put his hands in his pockets to keep from touching her while the plan formed with perfect clarity in his mind.

"What am I missing?" she asked.

"What's the first thing I asked you to do for me in Germany?"

"Give you the weapons and a transmitter."

He grinned. "After that."

Her eyebrows drew together in a small frown. "Follow the money."

"Exactly. Not the biologist or the lab. *The money*. Whelan isn't here to point out a fictitious buyer. He's here to make up for a lost payday and erase the one failure from his record. We can use that to our advantage."

"How can you be so sure without searching his financials? Without knowing who let him into the States?"

He didn't want to tell her he had Jason looking into those aspects. He also didn't want to tell her the other reason Whelan hated him. An old pain twisted in his gut. Truth was Thomas should have seen this coming. "If we ambush him here or here—" he reached around her, pointing to the most likely choke points on the one decent road in and out of Glenstone "—we can stop him and interrogate him before he makes another attempt on our lives."

"Interrogate or eliminate?"

"Interrogate. I intend to know which agent or agency bought his ridiculous story."

She leaned back and folded her arms across her chest. "Sounds to me like you're going against your own training."

"How so?"

"You're going in without several pertinent details."

"Trust me, Whelan is primarily money motivated. Someone is paying him to cause this havoc, which ties right in with the revenge he yearns for. Plus, we know he's not working alone."

She sat forward again. "You're assuming it was Whelan

with a driver who took a shot at us after the airport attempt failed."

"I am."

"Okay, let's work out a strategy to beat an ambush. But the results are on you."

Which was precisely what he wanted. He didn't want her—or anyone else—further embroiled in this mess. He trusted Grant to have warned Lucas about Whelan. He trusted Lucas to protect the wedding party. Now it was up to him to clear his name and protect Jo in the process.

"Great." They had a plan he felt could work. "Now let's go clear off the car so we're ready to move when the snowplow shows up."

"I thought you wanted to rehash the Isely mission."

"We can multitask." He was already sliding into his slightly charred sport coat and the gloves she'd bought for him last night. Eager, sure, but it also gave him that essential distance…from this intimate setting. "If we hurry, we might have time to dry out our shoes before we have to leave for Glenstone."

"Hmm." She slid into his overcoat. "You've given this a lot of thought."

"I have." More than she knew.

"When did you sleep?" Her hand fell lightly on his sleeve, but it was enough contact to stop him in his tracks. He felt himself getting lost in those dark eyes of hers again. If she gave any indication she was open to another kiss, that she still thought of those days in Austria or had any lingering feelings for him, he'd leap. But he couldn't think like that. Not until this was over anyway.

"Promise me something?"

Looking down into her face, he was ready to promise her anything. The realization scared him. "That depends."

"Whatever happens today, you'll let me keep watch tonight."

"Deal." He turned to the door, but she tugged him back.

"That isn't a promise."

"I'll sleep when we're done, Jo."

Her face, a vision of hope a moment ago, seemed to fade into something akin to disappointment. She withdrew her hand and he felt a chill, though he had yet to open the door.

"Jo—"

"I understand, Thomas. Truly I do." She looked away, then back. "Do you have the gun?"

"Yes. And it's loaded." He reached into his pocket. "Do you want the sedative?" He held it out, hoping the gesture would cheer her up, but her smile didn't even get half-way across her mouth and nowhere near putting a spark in her eyes.

"Keep it. I doubt it would work on a rogue bear, which is all the danger we're likely to run into before tonight."

He hoped she was right.

Outside, the mountain peaks that had been hidden by heavy snow clouds yesterday were in full glory today. He could just imagine how well things were going up at the resort. "You'll want sunglasses," he suggested to Jo, but she was already putting them on.

The bright sunshine was deceptive, giving the impression of warmth when it was still quite cold.

He tromped through the snow, taking a relieved glee in feeling like a kid again. He grinned over his shoulder. "Your mom picked a good spot. This hill is just begging for a sled. Is there one around?"

"Please. Do boys ever really grow up?"

"It's part of our charm."

"We can call it charm if you like."

"You disagree?" He watched her tread carefully through

the path he'd made earlier when he'd come out to dig the bullet free.

"Not if we're talking about you. You're quite charming, Director."

He chuckled, knowing her committee used less flattering terms when his name came up in discussion. "You're just saying that because I've been doing the cooking."

"A girl has to eat." With her arms outstretched she shoved snow from the hood of the car, which landed in a heap at his feet.

Her grin was feminine and wily and his reaction was stronger than he'd expected. He wanted to kiss that expression right off her face. The feelings, the startling attraction, should have faded long ago.

He thought of the last time he'd seen her, across a glossy conference table. There hadn't been a greater challenge to his self-control. Until last night.

"Are you trying to tell me you looked at this blank canvas and didn't think of making snow angels?" He worked on clearing the rest of the roof while she cleared the headlights and then shuffled around to clear the taillights and exhaust pipe.

"Because that's naturally what good little girls want to do in fresh snow?"

"You said as much once." In Germany as they'd looked out past the village and up to the white-topped mountains, she'd shared more than she probably meant to. More than he should have remembered.

That mission seemed like a lifetime away and just yesterday all at the same time. It was a strange sensation and not at all comfortable. He should be discussing the business of those days, not the pleasure.

"Do you think it's possible Whelan managed to get his hands on the real virus?"

He paused, knocking the snow from his gloves and dusting it off of his jeans. Thank goodness one of them still had the power of logical thought. "No. I'm sure the family always meant to double-cross the buyer."

"And you."

Thomas spread his hands. "Isely is not dealing bioweapons anymore, and that was the purpose of the trip."

"True." She was shuffling and stamping her feet in an effort to clear a path behind the car. "You called wrapping up Whelan a bonus."

Thomas smiled, thinking back. "For a quiet little town, it had a significant criminal element that week."

"As does Glenstone once you and Whelan are in town. If you give credence to rumor."

He laughed. "We ought to just build a snowman or a fort or something."

"Thomas."

"It would be a more efficient way to clear a path than what you're trying to do."

"You could come help me."

He nodded. "Or I could make snow angels."

"How about a whole choir of them right here?" She pointed to a spot near her that would help clear the path.

"Maybe." He reached down and scooped up a handful of snow, testing how well it packed. With a perfect snowball, he tossed it up a few inches, gauging the weight.

Her ruby lips parted. "No." She wagged a finger at him. "Don't you dare."

He let it fly, and tagged her shoulder as she struggled through the deep snow to get behind the shelter of the car.

"Thomas!"

"You didn't want to make a snowman or a fort."

He heard her grumbling about men being nothing but

overgrown boys, but he knew she was stockpiling ammunition and developing a counterattack strategy.

He wasn't wasting time either. He packed a few snowballs and cradled them in the crook of his arm as he waited to see what she would do.

The attack didn't come from the back of the car as he expected, it came from above and landed far too close. He looked skyward, squinting against the brightness, and nearly got a face full of snow. Clever woman was lobbing them over the car like grenades.

There was nothing for it but to charge ahead. He rounded the car and began pelting her with snowballs, dodging as she fired back. Amid the shrieks, vows of vengeance and laughter, he wasn't sure who had the most hits when she called for a truce a few minutes later.

"You're unarmed?" She was hidden behind the wide branches of a Douglas fir.

"Yes." And his jeans were cold and wet, clinging to his legs now that he'd stopped moving. "Let's go inside and warm up."

"Okay." She stepped out from the shelter of the tree and he found himself the victim of an ambush. Three snowballs smacked into his chest accompanied by her crow of victory.

Unable to let it stand and lose gracefully, he charged forward. Spurred by another shriek, he lunged and tackled her into a snowbank.

"I won," she declared.

"You're sure?" He had her pinned under his body. "Seems I have the advantage." Despite the layers of coats and clothing his body was remembering every hot, luscious curve of hers. Her cheeks were pink from the exertion and her lips rosy. He pushed her sunglasses up into her hair, needing to see her eyes.

The stark desire in those midnight depths fueled the needs surging to the surface. He kept his gaze locked with hers, praying she wouldn't stop him as he lowered his mouth to her sweet lips.

He told himself one more taste would be enough to carry him through. Through what defied definition as he lost all reason at that first contact.

It was simultaneously new and achingly familiar. He wanted to take his time and rush headlong into the next sensation. Only with her had he felt so much passion and so little control.

"Johara," he whispered reverently as he feathered kisses over her cheeks, jaw and finally her lips again. He couldn't remember why he had forced himself to walk away from her and at the moment it didn't matter. Couldn't matter. Right now, he just wanted to make up for lost time.

She drew his head closer, her lips parting in an unmistakable invitation. The snow was surely steaming away by the heat they generated as her velvet tongue dueled with his.

The cold was irrelevant and time seemed to stop. He thought even the earth moved. That was a first.

Her hands pushed at his shoulders and he eased back reluctantly.

"Snowplow."

"Huh?"

"Look." Her kiss-swollen lips curved into a smile. "It's the snowplow." She gave him another nudge and he rolled back then helped her to her feet.

He considered brushing the snow from her shapely bottom, but putting his hands on her again wouldn't be wise. It took more effort than it should have to shake off the passionate haze, and he let her take the lead as she approached the driver.

The plow was a heavy-duty pickup outfitted with a blade to push the snow to the side of the narrow road connecting the cabin to the rest of civilization.

Thomas wasn't sure if he should be grateful. At the moment he felt cheated.

Chapter Fourteen

9:30 a.m.

Jason had awakened with the sun, out of habit more than design, though he had been eager enough to leave the lumpy bed. Sleep had been in short supply after skimming the incriminating files on the flash drive he'd found in DeRossi's room.

As he'd dressed, he double-checked, then triple-checked the strength of the cell signal on his phone, relieved the networks were back up. He'd had just enough time to check out of the motel and hit up a drive-through for coffee. Then he could take the call from Lucas in the relative privacy of his car.

He made the call to the number on his cell display that matched the number in the message that had come back from the resort last night.

"Mr. Camp, this is Jason Grant."

"Morning, Grant." After a quick thank-you for the warning about Whelan, Lucas got to the point. "I'm sure you have other orders, but I'd like you to consider what I'm about to ask."

Jason was more than happy to listen to the man; he was a legend. As Lucas spoke, Jason's concerns gave way quickly to anticipation at the plan he outlined to protect the director.

"Sir, I'll head straight for Glenstone now. You should be aware I found information that the director is under an investigation."

"By whom?"

"The Initiative. An agent by the name of DeRossi intercepted him at the airport yesterday afternoon."

"DeRossi?"

"Yes, sir. The files I found are hard to believe." Jason worried the call had dropped again when the former deputy director didn't reply right away.

"Then don't believe them. Is DeRossi the person you referred to as Whelan's date?"

"No, sir. I believe there's another woman on the director's trail. I can't confirm her purpose or affiliations as of yet." He merged onto the Interstate while Lucas thought that through.

"I'm sending the Drakes to meet you. You realize I can't officially authorize any action, but I'm trusting the three of you to do whatever it takes to contain Whelan and protect the director. I'm certain we all want him safe and I need him here in time to walk his niece down the aisle."

Jason grinned. "We won't let you down, sir."

"Specialists never do."

As the call disconnected, Jason felt the spike in his energy level and knew it had nothing to do with the caffeine. He still didn't have all the facts, but he felt much better about this course of action. Thomas Casey respected and trusted Lucas Camp. That was all Jason needed to know to move forward with this plan.

Chapter Fifteen

"Good morning!" the snowplow driver called, leaning out of his window. "You folks doing okay up here?"

Thomas waved, but he let Jo do the talking.

"We're great, thanks," she replied, sending him an odd look. "We lost power last night, but there was plenty of firewood and the power was back on this morning."

"Good to know."

"Want some coffee or anything?"

"No, thanks," the driver declined. "I'm all set. I'll just clear a path here and be on my way."

"Thank you. I can't tell you how glad we are to see you." Jo looked immensely grateful they weren't going to be trapped here anymore.

"How are the other roads?" Thomas stepped up and put his arm around her shoulders, mostly to give the driver the impression they were a couple. Then again, they'd sure as hell been acting like one before he arrived.

"Clear as glass. Frosted glass anyway," he said with a chuckle at his joke. "You won't have any trouble getting down the mountain."

Thomas nodded. "Thanks again."

"Oh, nearly forgot." The driver reached over to the passenger seat and pulled up a small box. "This came into the office." He jerked his chin at Jo. "Tried to deliver this the other day, but you weren't in and I didn't want to leave it just sitting out. It's marked fragile."

Jo tensed. "Addressed to me?"

"No, just the cabin number, but seeing as you were the only one booked for this month we figured…"

"Appreciate it." Gingerly, she accepted the package and stepped away from the truck.

She didn't return to Thomas's side. He assumed she shared his concern that this little surprise was from Whelan.

But how the hell would he know to look here? And if he suspected they were here last night why not make a move?

That one was pretty easy to answer really, Thomas decided. Whelan didn't just want to take him out—he wanted to take him all the way down.

With a tap to the bill of his ball cap, the driver cleared the snow from behind the SUV and headed back down the road.

When the rumble of the engine faded, Thomas and Jo stared at each other.

"Thoughts?"

He had several, not the least of which was how far she might be able to toss that package into the trees. "Someone has far better access than they should."

"Agreed."

He walked toward her, wincing when she twitched. "Careful."

"I'm fine. You should stay back."

"That's not going to happen." He took another step.

"Thomas, please." She raised the box to her face. "It doesn't smell like oranges."

"Hooray," he deadpanned. "Now set it down and come here."

"Just a second." She was slowly examining the package from every angle. "There's a loose flap."

"For God's sake, Jo, put the box down."

"What if it's the virus? Or a clue that can clear you?"

He strode forward, heedless of the irritated glare she shot him. "And it could just as easily be another bomb that will kill us both."

He looked at the label and judged it useless. It could have been printed from any computer at any given time, and covered with clear packing tape, recovering a fingerprint was a lost cause.

"I don't think so," she said. "It's been rattling around in his truck, it can't be that volatile."

She had a point, but that didn't mean he had to acknowledge it. "Show me this loose flap."

"Right here." She shifted the box so he had a better look. "Isn't that the same number that was on the German euro?"

"Yes."

"It's a Washington, D.C., phone number, right?"

"Yes."

"We need to find a phone and call it."

"No point."

"Why not?"

"It's Deputy Director Holt's private line."

She gasped. "He's behind this setup?"

"We don't know that." He shook his head, not wanting to believe it. If the man had been turned, the whole team was at risk. His stomach rolled at the deadly potential if Holt had shifted his loyalty. Just because Thomas didn't want to accept it, didn't mean it wasn't possible.

"What're you thinking?" she prompted. She was getting nervous; he could hear it in her voice.

"I'm supposedly selling bio-weapons on the side." They both knew that wasn't true. Still, he felt like he had to warn

Lucas. Holt had access and the reliable resources to dig up what he couldn't find on his own. "It looks bad, but it doesn't make sense. What's Holt's play here?"

"Control of Mission Recovery," she said with a tone that implied he was a dunce for not thinking of it himself.

"He's going to get that soon enough when I retire anyway."

"You're planning to retire?"

"Someday," he hedged, not wanting to get into that discussion here and now. "And Holt knows that."

"Something, anything could have upped his timeline." She shivered.

He didn't want her catching cold. This wrinkle meant they would both have to be at their best to squeeze out with their lives and reputations. "We'll discuss this inside. Leave that here."

"We need to open it."

This was the wrong time for her to exhibit the famous DeRossi tenacity. He sighed. "We will. After we go inside, warm up and develop an exit strategy. In light of the circumstances, I'm not opening a strange package until I know we can mitigate any consequences."

"Okay. I'll just leave it here under the tree."

He didn't breathe easy until they were safely inside the house and the cabin door closed against the mysterious package.

She shrugged out of his overcoat. "What do you think it is?"

"It could be anything," he said, hanging both coats on the peg by the door. "You should change out of those wet clothes."

"In a minute. You're worried it is something specific."

She was like a dog with a bone and he knew he wouldn't shake her loose. "It could be a beacon, a bomb, or like you said, it could be the virus I thought I confiscated five years ago."

"If it's the virus, leaving it out there isn't smart." She rubbed her arms.

Seeing her chilled, he considered warming her up with more kisses, but that look in her eyes told him she wouldn't be so easily distracted. The fun was over for today. Truth was neither one of them could afford to be distracted right now. "I'll keep watch and put out the fire. Go change into dry clothes. We should leave as soon as possible."

She started down the hallway and stopped short. "If it is a bomb, can you defuse it?"

"Can you?"

She shook her head. "Who's your best explosives expert?"

He didn't want to answer that. All of his Specialists were trained in what he considered essential skills for fieldwork. At the moment, among the active roster at Mission Recovery, Holt was the most qualified to deal with an IED. That detail did nothing to ease his mind. "The better question is where my best explosives experts are. And the answer would be too far away to help."

"Is there anyone among the wedding party who—"

It was a fair question and probably the smart thing to do. But this was his problem and he meant to resolve it without taking that step. "I am not going to disrupt the festivities or worry Casey or anyone else with that kind of request."

"I see."

He didn't like the sound of that reply, or the sadness weighing those two little words. "As you said, it's probably not a bomb since it's been rattling around in a truck for who knows how long," he said defensively.

"Uh-huh."

"Go change," he barked. "Before you catch pneumonia."

"Don't you go out there without me," she snapped back, with an equal bite in her voice.

"I promise." He looked up. It wasn't quite what he'd meant to say. But the effect was worth the potential error. Judging by her expression, his choice of words startled her, then a smile bloomed across her face.

Mussed from his kisses, her clothes soaked in places due to the snow, she remained a breathtaking beauty. Helpless to do otherwise, he watched her walk away until she disappeared into the bedroom.

Only then did he turn back to the hearth and smother the fire burning low. As he broke apart the logs, recent events ran through his mind a few times.

It might defy common sense, but he just couldn't lay all of this on Holt. Not without a clear motive or proof beyond the convenient and circumstantial evidence.

He stared out the window, even as he heard Jo return to the front room.

"Did I miss anything?"

"No."

"You should change clothes, too."

"I'll dry in the car." He wanted to get away from here, with or without the package, before anything bad happened to the cabin her mother left her. He remembered that she'd spoken so fondly of her mother. Jo didn't have any family left now. He didn't want bad memories ruining her obvious love for this place. "I think the sooner we go the better."

She nodded. "I figured as much." She stepped aside to gather her tablet and he noticed she'd wheeled out the suitcase she'd brought for him. He resisted the urge to thank her. Bringing him clothing had been thoughtful, but it was still on the unnerving side to think of her rifling through his apartment.

"How did you bypass my security system?"

"I didn't have to."

"I beg your pardon?"

"For the search, I went in when you were at the gym."

He shook his head. It was the only time he didn't set the alarm. The gym was in his building, didn't seem necessary. How could she know him so well? "I can't believe I didn't miss my own clothes."

"I didn't steal your laundry, Thomas. I just went through your credit card statement and then reordered a few of the same items you most recently purchased."

"My credit card statement," he echoed, dumbfounded.

"The gift for the newlyweds was inspired."

Despite everything, her praise on that score made him feel better. He'd worried that ordering a painted portrait of Casey and Levi's engagement photo had been a lame idea. Her support and how it eased his mind startled him. Why was he feeling anything but anger over her intrusion into his personal life?

Because for some inexplicable reason, he saw her differently from other agents he'd worked with. He'd learned quickly to value her observations and opinion. Just because she'd gone to the Initiative when he'd invited her to Mission Recovery…get past it. Going there wouldn't change a damned thing.

"Ease up, Thomas. It wasn't fraud. I paid with my own card."

"So I should thank you?"

She opened her mouth and promptly snapped it shut again, clearly rethinking her reply. The smile that followed wasn't anything close to friendly. "Think of it as belated Christmas and birthday all wrapped up together."

"In one neatly packed suitcase."

"And five years too late. Forgive me." She took a step closer and instinctively he backed away from the irritation sparking in her dark eyes. "I promise never to think of your comfort again."

"My comfort? You planned an abduction here, Jo." Why was he starting a fight? Maybe so he wouldn't be so damned tempted to throw her across that couch and show her what he really wanted. They had at least one killer after them and there was an unknown package only a few feet away. Where the hell was his head?

"An abduction!" She turned the air blue with a cloud of Italian curses. He was somewhat surprised to find himself still standing when she stopped. "I wanted a conversation, an open dialogue so I could help you." She planted her hands on her hips. "Thomas Casey, you don't know the full extent of what I planned and as of now you never will."

He believed her and marveled at the sudden emptiness in his chest. Was it regret? He'd spent his career making tough choices, but never regretting anything. Except walking away from her. Her pain was obvious, pain he'd caused.

More regret.

"Jo, I'm sorry. When we get out of this—"

She lurched forward, covering his mouth with her hand. "Listen," she whispered, pointing to the ceiling.

He heard it then, the *whump-whump* of a helicopter rotor. He watched her expression, knowing they were both ticking off the plausible reasons it was in the area. Traffic. Unlikely since this area of the mountain had never been populated enough to create congestion. Weather, but he dismissed that, too, as news agencies would be focused on getting shots of the more popular ski resorts. Out here in the wilderness, he couldn't come up with anything worthy enough to warrant a chopper—other than the two of them.

"Beacon," they said at the same time. They both turned toward the window and the package under the tree.

"Any way out? Place to hide?"

She shook her head. "No on both counts."

The nine-millimeter and one extra clip wasn't enough to make a stand. They couldn't make it out on foot. Not only would they leave a clear trail in the deep snow, but they also didn't have the gear to make hiking practical. Even on adrenaline, neither of them had the stamina to keep up a pace that would outdistance the enemy in these conditions. Making a run for it in the car was their only chance.

"Keys," he demanded. She tossed them his way. "I'll start the car. You get the package."

He could see she wanted to argue. "We have to lead them away from here." He couldn't bear it if her mother's cabin were destroyed in the witch hunt aimed at him.

"They'll tear it up anyway," she protested as if she'd read his mind.

"Just do it."

He slung her duffel bag across his chest and she did the same with her purse. Opening the door, they raced across the snow that had been a playground a mere hour ago.

This time they were running for their lives.

He tossed the luggage into the back, slammed the door and then leaped into the driver's seat. Stabbing the key into the ignition, he threw the car into Reverse and whipped around to put Jo closer to the passenger door.

She scrambled inside, dumping her purse and the package on the floor at her feet so she could secure her seat belt.

He checked the gas gauge, hoping the repair would hold up as he went tearing down the narrow mountain road.

"What's the plan?"

He didn't know. It wasn't the first time he had to wing it, but this time felt more important. It wasn't just a matter of national security or his professional pride. There was more on the line now. Casey and Levi. His sister and Lucas and his family. His team. Jo. All of them were at risk because someone wanted to add his funeral to the weekend festivities.

He had news for that someone: he wasn't going down easy.

He rolled down the windows and turned off the heater to make it easier to hear the helicopter.

"It's getting closer," he said. "Can you identify it?"

She listened and twisted around in her seat, trying to get eyes on it while he did his best to keep them on the road in the lousy conditions.

"Definitely not civilian."

He agreed. The taller trees obscured their view, but they also reacted to the rotor wash. "Behind us." The treetops were bowing. "Right flank."

"Got it," she said, straining against the seat belt as he took a hairpin turn too quickly. "Oh, no."

"What?" But he thought he knew.

"It's a Russian Hind."

"Good."

"What? You do have a death wish."

"Not as maneuverable. Very memorable." And not American meant privately contracted or a European enemy. If Holt were involved he could have mustered U.S. equipment without too much paperwork, especially here in the backyard of both the Air Force and NORAD.

But analysis took a backseat to evasion as a tree exploded in front of them.

"I should have rented an up-armored Hummer," she muttered as they bounced around and through the debris.

"Is that an available option package?"

After a stunned pause, she laughed. "Only at select dealerships."

"In Idaho or Montana," he joked, stomping on the gas as they hit an exposed straight stretch of road.

Her laughter was a welcome counterpoint to the persistent rotors bearing down on them.

"How can you joke at a time like this?"

"I'm human." And he'd rather go out laughing than crying. "Open up that package."

She hurried to oblige and still preserve as much evidence as possible, slicing the tape at the seams with her fingernail. "If this beacon blows up, it's been a pleasure serving with you."

"Same goes. But it won't."

He felt the air change as the helicopter pilot had to lift, compensating for a thicker stand of trees. It was a welcome reprieve. They were almost to the state road.

He slowed down, taking advantage of the cover though it wouldn't buy them much more than a few seconds. "Glenstone or Denver?"

"Has to be Denver."

Thomas wasn't so sure.

"Better cover."

"But—" They were closer to Glenstone. He had to believe even a small population would be a deterrent to the shooter in the helicopter. It was going to be a long, lonely stretch of two-lane highway before they met the Interstate.

"They expect us to head to Glenstone," she added. "For both the sale and the wedding. In Denver we can—"

The menacing roar of the helicopter engine and rotors filled the air. Bullets tore up the roadway behind them. He floored it again and when he reached the state highway, he turned toward Denver. "Maybe we'll get lucky and a crosswind will force him down."

"I know for a fact Director Casey has never relied on luck."

"That's because luck's a fickle b—" Jo's exclamation cut him off. "What now?"

She held up the box and he swore at the sight of the glaring red light blinking on a small transmitter and a vial that looked all too familiar. A neatly folded note was tucked between the two.

If he'd harbored any doubts about a setup, they were gone now. "Assuming that's the real stuff in that vial, why bother when they're determined to make me dead?"

"Evidence," she said. "Ties it up in a neat bow for whoever investigates why they took lethal action against a man of your standing."

She was right. He downshifted, managed the turn and prayed for a crosswind as they burst into a wide-open stretch of slushy, sunlit road. He nearly cheered when he saw an eighteen-wheeler and a couple of other cars heading their way.

He slowed down, hoping the gunner in the chopper was smart enough to avoid witnesses.

"What does the note say?"

She removed and opened it tentatively. "'Enjoy your retirement.'"

"Oh, I will. When it's my decision," he growled.

He almost pulled a U-turn in the middle of the winding road, ready to tear apart Glenstone until he found Whelan and shook the truth out of him.

"He's out over the river," Jo reported.

Thomas jerked his thoughts away from the dark but satisfying vision of interrogating Whelan again. He had other things to think about. Like how to lose the helicopter shadowing their movements. There were options; he just had to find the right one.

"Forget that a minute." He tapped the map tucked into the cup holder in the console between them. "Tell me what's coming up."

She rattled off names of roads, a few he recalled from

last night. "Give me a road with a creek and a blind corner."

"You don't ask for much, do you?"

He actually laughed. "You hadn't heard the rumors of my exhausting standards?"

She snorted. "I always thought they were exaggerations."

Traffic slowed and Thomas was forced to match the pace or cause trouble for innocent bystanders. The helicopter swooped right over them. "He's looking for a fast resolution. Failing a divine intervention, we need cover."

"This next intersection leads out to Eagle Creek."

He judged the terrain from his current position and pulled over to turn left at the light. It looked like this way would have more tree cover.

"Is there really a creek?"

"Yes. The road runs alongside for a bit."

"How long?"

"Looks like about ten miles."

"Great. Do you have a plastic zipper bag?"

"Yes. The one I used to get through airport security." She set the open box aside and dug into the depths of her oversize purse. "Got it."

Both of them looked skyward as the sound of the rotors grew louder. The big attack helicopter had found the firing solution. Staying low, the pilot followed the open space of the road, giving the gunner a good line of sight.

"Thomas?"

He heard the doubt and fear in that one word, hated that he'd put her in this position. An unfamiliar worry that he couldn't pull this one out churned in his gut. "Not very friendly looking this close, huh?"

"Not at all," she agreed.

"Where's a surface-to-air missile when you need one?"

She didn't laugh this time and he couldn't blame her. With the reptilian paint job and the wings loaded with armament, the helicopter looked exactly like what it was: a mean, deadly machine.

"That was the point of the design." He started rambling, offering a short lesson on the design history as a distraction, hoping cold logic would help somehow. In truth, her fear was more than justified. They were sitting ducks, stuck in the left turn lane just waiting for the fatal bullet.

"They won't shoot in front of all these witnesses," Jo said.

He disagreed with her, but he didn't say it. Whoever wanted him dead had a clear and effective exit strategy. The pilot and gunner wouldn't care about a few bystanders on the ground who would never be able to identify the shooter or accurately describe the helicopter. Thomas muttered curses at the light and the cars in front of him until the light finally changed and traffic started moving. He followed the string of cars through the intersection and gave thanks for the sudden shadows of the tall trees on either side of the road.

"Careful of the vial, put the beacon in the plastic bag," he said. "Now we just need an overlook or something where we can get close to the creek."

The helicopter was never out of earshot, and Thomas envisioned the pilot swinging back and forth over the road, tracking the beacon but unable to get eyes on them.

"There!" Jo pointed to an overlook sign, and in the lighter traffic he was able to pull over to the shoulder and quickly pull to a stop.

Maybe luck was on their side as the lot was currently clear of other travelers.

He held out his hand for the bag and she gave it to him. "Back the car into the trees while I take care of this."

He sneered at the pesky flashing light and double-checked the seal on his way to the waterway. With a silent prayer he flung the bag toward the water.

He watched just long enough to see it land in the water and bob along with the modest current. Floating the beacon downstream was a sucker's bet at best, but if it bought them a few moments of peace, he'd take it.

Hearing the helicopter circling back, he took cover under the low-hanging limbs of a tree. Snow skittered down his collar, melting in a bitter-cold trickle between his shirt and his skin. But he didn't so much as blink while he waited for the helicopter to pass by. The mottled gray-green beast hovered in the area for a tension-filled eternity before moving on.

Jogging back to the car, he shook the remaining snow out of his jacket. "Move over," he said, gesturing for her to shift out of the driver's seat.

"Where to now?" She buckled up and looked at him expectantly. "Denver or Glenstone. We could get this tested in the city."

"Glenstone," he replied, moving cautiously into the traffic lane. "What's in the vial doesn't matter as long as we control it."

"Then why not just head on up to the lodge?"

He shook his head. Eager as he was to spend time with Casey and Cecelia, he hadn't forgotten the very real threat of an angry explosives expert. "Only after Whelan's in custody."

She peered up at the sky, but the view was clear and the only sounds were normal traffic. "How long before they realize they've lost us?"

"As they say in poker, they've been rivered. Hopefully long enough to get us safely into Glenstone."

Anticipating his next request, she pulled out the map. "Let me find an alternate route."

He reached across the seat and gave her hand a squeeze. She couldn't know how much he needed to touch her, to assure himself they'd pull this off. "Thank you for not believing the worst of me."

"You as a traitor is only possible in an alternate reality. I'm well aware you're no saint," she said with a ghost of a smile. "But hero certainly applies after you saved us from Godzilla-copter."

He brought his hand back to the steering wheel, needing the distance. The feelings rushing through him now were fierce and he wasn't sure he could handle them and focus his attention where it needed to be. "It's a long shot he'll stay gone. They know where we were and where we're headed."

Jo STUDIED THOMAS'S profile; as capable as he was, the tension of the chase showed in his white knuckles and clenched jaw. "We can change where we're headed."

"If we don't show up at Glenstone, Whelan's sure to go to the resort. I can't risk him hurting anyone there to draw me out."

"I sent an email about the Hind while you were tossing the beacon."

"Why?"

"You're not the only one with contacts."

"Grant will be enough help."

"You trust him? After all of this? If someone can send a beacon to my mother's cabin and order a Russian gunship to take us out, I think it's high time I called on one of my contacts."

"You'll be in enough trouble as it is, when the committee realizes you've helped me."

He was right. They would never approve of how she'd handled this. "I think it's safe to say the committee believes we're in this together. Which is one reason I used my primary account to report a helicopter firing on civilians to an old Air Force buddy."

"He didn't fire on civilians, just us."

"Hmm. I thought your primary purpose for being in Colorado was vacation."

"That's a fine line you're dancing on."

"Right. Because you never blur those edges."

"Contacts don't like being used, Jo."

She studied the map, looking for another way into Glenstone. It kept her from making eye contact with him. "Well, if you can't burn a bridge for a friend, what's the point?"

"We're friends?"

She refused to dignify that with any comment. She didn't know how to answer. Her heart ached with love for him, but it was clear he was only interested in more of the physical. He still hadn't shown her any real trust. This was the worst possible time and place to have those feelings but it was beyond her control...very much like this situation. Any of myriad agents she'd worked with or investigated could have enjoyed an affair in the Alps for what it was: a good time.

She'd had five years to review and reassess those brief days. With anyone else it would have been a good time and fond memories. But Jo had felt so much more with Thomas. That had been the personal angle she'd set out to accomplish on this very delicate assignment, and now she knew friends—even friends with benefits—wouldn't be enough for her.

Thomas held a piece of her heart she'd never expected to lose. It was as simple and as complicated as that.

"Too bad we can't test this virus on the pilot once the Air Force forces him to land."

Thomas's deep laugh loosened the knots in her stomach that had been twisting around since that kiss. She touched her lips, remembering. Being trapped between his hot body and the cold snow had been the most delicious sensation. There wasn't much point denying it, she just had to figure out how to get over it. Too bad she didn't have the first clue.

The desire was there, on a consistent simmer between them. All it needed was a private opportunity to boil over again. They'd have that tonight—provided they lived that long.

Yes, she'd wanted to test the staying power of the passion they'd shared five years ago. Fool that she was, now that it was too late, she realized seizing that opportunity would only end in heartache. He hadn't changed. She wasn't sure he was capable of trusting anyone other than himself.

"Any options?"

"No." She wanted to crumple the map into a tiny ball and toss it out the window. "It's a mountain. One road straight through town. Smaller streets branch off, but as you said, 'choke point.'"

"We need to get ahead of this."

She pointed to the clock on the dash. "If the Hind is still in the area, he's surely reported losing us by now. And the Air Force will be looking for him."

"Not if the beacon's still transmitting."

"The creek and road don't run concurrent forever. I'm pretty sure they don't think we've suddenly decided to go kayaking."

"No, but we've divided their attention," he said. "Are you willing to send a text message from your tablet?"

"Sure. But if someone in my office or yours is monitoring the account, they'll know."

"I'm counting on it."

"The Glenstone hotel room isn't enough bait?"

His smile was cryptic as he dictated the message.

"Received a better offer. Will cut you in, if you call off the wolf."

Arguing was pointless, so she kept quiet and sent it anyway. That was an inflammatory text the Initiative would be happy to use against him. She didn't recognize the number he had her send it to, but she trusted him. He slowed down, making the turn into a gas station.

"Are we leaking fuel again?"

"No, just a normal fill-up." He parked by a pump and gave her an easy smile. "Would you please go ask about decent restaurants around here?"

She knew from the map there weren't any real stops between here and Glenstone. He was stalling. As she climbed out of the car, she pushed aside the hurt that he wouldn't share the details of the latest twist he'd worked up.

Knowing he wanted her face to show up on surveillance, she pasted on a wide smile and strolled inside.

She'd heard of leaving breadcrumbs, but this was ridiculous. It felt more like leaving a trail of neon signs with blinking arrows, especially after so much training on how to fit in, or better yet, disappear.

A few minutes later Thomas leveled his attention on her as she approached. "Restaurants?"

"There's a mom-and-pop place just up the road. Have you chosen the car yet?" She folded her arms and leaned against the driver's door. "Probably better to do it here than at the diner."

"I beg your pardon?"

"You want to steal a car so we can slip past the choke

point." He gave her what she had to assume he considered his innocent look. "That's not going to work."

"You'd rather go into an ambush with a weak gas tank?"

"I meant the innocent routine. Changing cars makes sense. Changing. Not stealing."

"We don't have time to drive back to Denver and swap out the rental."

"Why not? It's not yet noon and the roads and sky are clear."

He leaned close, caging her between his strong arms. She resisted the urge to push him away, knowing if she touched him again, her waning self-control would simply evaporate. Still, she longed to touch him, to slide her hands under the layers and rediscover the hard planes and warm skin.

"The sky isn't exactly clear."

What? She dragged her thoughts out of the sensual haze. Distraction killed more agents than bullets and with an unknown enemy with too much access, they couldn't afford mistakes here.

She jerked her chin, refusing to back down no matter how he tried to cow her. "You said it yourself." Her gaze dropped to his mouth and she licked her lips. *Mission first, man later.* Why couldn't she remember that? "They expect us to head toward the resort. However they got that euro into the car, they didn't put a GPS tag on the vehicle or they would have been on top of me—us—last night."

Based on the way his blue eyes flashed with desire, it might have been the wrong choice of words. It certainly conjured a few sexy images in her mind.

"The weather was an equalizer."

"Yes, but we weren't attacked until the beacon arrived."

"Along with the virus, to complete the setup, as you

pointed out. Which indicates they had an idea where we would land last night."

She saw the words as much as she heard them with her gaze locked on his mouth. She wanted to argue that no one in her contacts knew about the cabin but the memory of the heat, the taste of him when his tongue had stroked against hers had her pulse skipping. She knew if she leaned forward, if he did, they'd be right back in that snowbank, the rest of the world a forgotten blur.

The gas pump shut off with a startling *thunk* and she realized they'd resolved nothing.

He turned away to cap the tank and deal with the pump and she rounded the hood to the passenger side of the car, hoping she didn't look like a scared mouse scurrying away from the cat.

Too late, she understood the problem was her lack of fear when it came to Thomas Casey. Five years ago, her steadfast belief in his ability in the field negated any fears she'd harbored about her involvement in the mission itself. She'd trusted him completely with her life on the job. Knowing it would only be temporary she'd trusted him with her body, and yet somehow she'd let him walk out with her heart. He'd owned it ever since and right now she couldn't see any way of getting back control over the traitorous organ.

Now, though she might be the only person in active service to the government who still believed in his integrity and patriotism, he didn't and, quite likely couldn't, return that trust. Still, he needed her this time almost as much as she had needed him before. And maybe she needed him in this far more than she realized.

Unless they both survived and could prove the truth... they were done.

As he pulled away from the gas pump he startled her by turning back toward the city. "What about being bait?"

"I've decided you're right. Charging straight into Glenstone is exactly what they expect me to do. Besides, the wedding itself is most important and if we don't finish this..." His voice trailed off, his eyes tracking the sky. "If I don't show up for the ceremony tomorrow night, Casey will kill me herself."

Jo tucked the tablet into her purse. "Head back to the airport. I have another car parked in the garage."

"I think I'd rather get a cab."

She laughed at his overdone expression of horror and she couldn't resist the devious sparkle in his eyes. "That's not a bad idea."

"It would get us past the choke point."

"And we'd be in Glenstone to keep an eye on Whelan," she said. Along with whomever he'd sent the message to. Knowing he wasn't ready to tell her, she didn't waste her breath with more questions.

At this point, she was just along for the ride.

Right...if she told herself that enough times maybe she would believe it.

She was here for him....

Chapter Sixteen

Glenstone Lodge

From the shade of the wide porch on the south side of the lodge, Victoria watched the wedding party tumble around in the fresh snow. The sun was shining and the air had a fresh bite. If not for the foot of snow, it was the perfect fall weather Casey had anticipated when she'd booked the resort for the long weekend celebration.

"It's so beautiful. Almost like the mountain wanted to dress for the occasion," she said to Cecelia, the mother of the bride.

"Keep that lovely sentiment ready to apply to a panicked bride-to-be."

The snowball fight might have been ruthless had the children not been there, but it was no less entertaining for the safety precautions. There had been the inevitable battle of the sexes, and even she and Cecelia had gotten swept into that frenzy for a short time. Now they were both content to sit with piping hot cocoa and supervise the construction of a carefully designed snow fort.

Cecelia checked her watch. "Casey is due to ask about her uncle in another two minutes."

Victoria gaped. "You've set your watch by her?"

The mother of the bride smiled. "Pretty much. I know

my brother will make it, but at the moment I'd like to wring his neck."

"Understandable," Victoria said with a soft chuckle. "You can take it out on him during the reception."

"Mmm. Something to look forward to. I appreciate your optimism."

"Optimism?"

"Thomas has always been dedicated to his career and I admire him for it." The chair creaked as she shifted. "Please don't misunderstand. I know he sees his work as an extension of his responsibility to the family, but there are times when nothing can excuse a personal absence."

Victoria knew precisely what she meant and took no offense at Cecelia's concerns. "Thomas has good people on his team. Lucas told me he—"

"Are we talking about Uncle Thomas?" Casey knocked the snow from her mittens.

"Yes," Victoria answered with a smile. "I was just telling your mother that whatever is keeping him, he won't miss your special day."

Casey met Victoria's gaze. "You'd tell me if there was something serious, right?"

"Absolutely." Victoria waved at a giggling cherubic face peeping up out of a snow tower. Luke, her grandson, was so precious. Jim and Tasha were around here somewhere. Those kids kept them on their toes. "The weather presented an unexpected problem, but the staff assured Lucas earlier if he isn't in a car that can make the drive up from Glenstone," Victoria assured her, "they can provide transportation."

"Good. I was going to ask if Levi should go into Denver and pick him up."

"No one needs to go anywhere. Least of all the groom," Cecelia said. "Go on and play."

"Mom," Casey said, affecting a perfect, childlike pout.

Victoria thought it must have been a challenge for her parents to resist that expression when she'd been a little girl. As a trained CIA agent herself, Cecelia likely would have better success going up against a staunch enemy.

"Go on," Cecelia repeated. "You'll know as soon as we do about your uncle's arrival. Enjoy yourself before it's time to get nervous for the rehearsal."

"I'm not the least bit nervous. I've surrounded myself with bridal armor chi," Casey said, beaming as only a happy bride-to-be can. "I'd even wish the ceremony was tonight if Uncle Thomas was here."

"He won't miss it." Cecelia made a shooing motion. "Go on."

"Fine." Casey kissed her mother on the cheek then swiped a finger though the whipped cream topping her mug.

Cecelia laughed. "Levi has no idea what a menace you are."

Casey grinned. "Of course he does."

Victoria thought the same thing as Casey dashed off to find her fiancé. Levi was a fine young man from a good family. He would cherish that young lady.

"Whatever is keeping Thomas, he won't let it ruin her big day," Victoria said when Casey was out of earshot. "He has good people dealing with any serious business. I'm sure this is just a transportation problem."

But she wasn't thinking of Thomas's Specialists, she was thinking of her husband's efforts to protect the wedding party. Since the arrival of the note last night, they'd been meeting quietly with several of the investigators in attendance. They'd developed a watch schedule and were keeping a keen eye on the personnel and deliveries to and from their secluded retreat.

If this Whelan character planned to threaten them, he'd find them prepared. Once more she prayed Thomas was equally prepared. She couldn't imagine her husband's grief if something were to happen to his best friend. Having dealt with more than her fair share of loss, she didn't want bleak memories to mar this special time for Cecelia or Casey.

The distinct sound of her husband's cane on the wooden planks of the porch floor drew her attention away from the group romping in the snow. She turned, hoping to catch his unguarded expression. She should have known better. His smile was warm, but his eyes were shaded by sunglasses, an effective shield. He would know she wasn't alone and wouldn't risk creating more worry than already floated on the thin air.

"There's a perfectly good fire going inside," he said after greeting Cecelia. "If you've had enough fun out here."

"I suppose sitting with you by the fire would be fair consolation after the girls trounced you boys in the snowball fight," Victoria teased. It would be a long time before she let him forget that victory.

"Your pity is appreciated," he replied with a deep bow.

She couldn't help it; the man charmed her no matter the circumstances. "You're welcome to join us," she said to Cecelia.

"No, thank you. I'm perfectly content right here." She patted the camera on the arm of the chair. "I want to get pictures of the finished fort."

Victoria walked away on Lucas's arm, wondering what news he didn't want to share in front of the mother of the bride. "She knows something is wrong. So does Casey."

"That's no shock. They're intelligent women and highly trained professionals," Lucas said.

Victoria could feel the tension in his arm, knew he

was starting to worry. She let him help her out of her coat when they reached the sitting room and settled in front of the fire. While several questions ran through her head, she knew he wouldn't tell her anything until he was ready.

He removed his sunglasses, confirming her suspicions that his reasons for wearing them went beyond the bright sunshine glaring off the snow.

"He won't make the rehearsal," he stated without preamble.

Victoria glanced at her watch. "There are hours yet."

Lucas shook his head. "We have to make a plan in case he can't shake this."

She didn't want to believe he was giving up, but the resignation was clear on his face. The sadness was already tugging at the corners of his mouth. "You're talking about Thomas Casey. He's second only to you in ability to get out of trouble."

The tension eased as Lucas's mouth tipped into a half smile. "We'll have to wait and see. I know he's determined and that's a good thing. But I'd feel better if I could talk with him."

"He'll be here." It was starting to feel like a mantra. "Does Holt have any relevant news?"

"No. But the Specialist who warned us about Whelan mentioned an Initiative investigation," he said quietly. "They suspect Thomas of treason. I've sent the Drakes out to help."

Victoria barely smothered her reaction. Treason and Thomas Casey were as opposite as the north and south poles. "Did he give you a name or anything we can work with?"

"Agent DeRossi is all I have." Lucas leaned on his cane. "Whatever he's dealing with, I fear it falls to us to keep the bride calm."

Victoria smiled and reached over to catch his hand with hers. "I've talked with Levi and her maid of honor. She's steady and confident her uncle will come through."

"I know."

Lucas had several reasons to know and appreciate Casey's nerves. Not only was he the girl's godfather, but also he'd trusted her with a task he'd kept secret from Victoria. She couldn't throw stones, as she'd secretly sent Levi into the field for the same purpose.

That mission had resolved a security issue threatening Lucas and Victoria as well as the Colby Agency. It had also brought Casey and Levi together.

"Casey offered to make a call."

"I can't imagine the CIA's involvement would be wise at this point," Victoria said.

Lucas nodded slowly. "I talked her out of it."

Knowing Casey, Victoria wasn't so sure the girl had really given up the idea of sending someone to assist her uncle. Saying so wouldn't ease her husband's concern, however, so she kept it to herself. For now.

"Has she asked you to fill in for Thomas at the rehearsal?"

He shook his head. "I changed the subject before she could ask. He'll be here."

"Yes, he will."

"Only one thing would keep him away."

A heavy silence fell between them and the fire couldn't touch the chill of potential disaster.

Victoria was relieved to hear the voices and booted feet when several of the wedding guests tromped in from outside.

They needed the happy distraction.

Chapter Seventeen

6:30 p.m.

From the wide glass windows of the suite, Lucas glowered down at the empty driveway as if he could make Thomas show up by sheer willpower alone.

He'd had far too much time to dwell on the parts of this nasty business to which he was privy.

"It's a setup," he grumbled. The idea that anyone could accuse Thomas of treason after all he'd given up in service for his country was laughable. But very few people had the clearance to read his file and understand the joke. Nine out of ten of Thomas's efforts in the field would be locked down with a classified label until the end of time. And the tenth would forever be buried deep in the archives of "never happened."

"Of course it is," Victoria said, stepping up beside him.

The warmth of her arms sliding around his waist was a balm to his senses. They were a good team and he was more grateful every day that they had each other. Yet, having her near only emphasized just how alone Thomas was out there.

"If he could just get up here, we could help him."

"Relax," she said. "You've done all you can. They'll find a way to clear his name."

He turned within her embrace and cupped her chin. "You're an optimist."

"So I've been told. I always considered myself a pragmatist. Optimism must be a side effect of our consistent success rate." She smiled, raising his hand to her lips and kissing his palm. "Doesn't make me wrong."

"No. It doesn't," he admitted. "Why are you so sure when I have so many doubts?"

"Intuition."

"Hmph." He struggled against the helpless feeling lodged in his chest.

"Aside from intuition, there is the cold hard truth that Thomas isn't capable of treason. Which means, setup or not, he will find a way to prevail."

"Before tomorrow's ceremony." Lucas hoped.

She reached out and smoothed his tie. "Nothing like a deadline to inspire some people."

He felt himself smiling, despite his misgivings. "We have the most talented investigators in the world under this roof. There should be more we can do."

"We're as prepared as we can be." She stepped back, adjusted the pendant at her throat. "We have to wait it out."

He thought of the men and women, here with spouses and children to celebrate Casey and Levi, and he understood what she wasn't saying. If a madman who liked to blow things up planned a strike against Thomas, the wedding was the perfect target to cause the most emotional damage and retire the most influential and revered man in the spy business.

As close as he and Thomas were, not even Lucas knew an enemy who would make such a bold and diabolical play.

His wife was right. They needed everyone on site alert and in protective mode to prevent a deadly assault on the wedding. As much as it grated against his instincts, he would have to trust Specialist Grant and the Drakes to help Thomas out without backup from him.

"I should have insisted he rent skis instead of staying in Denver last night."

"That's absurd."

"Only if it had failed." He smiled at her exasperated expression. Somehow it made him feel a little better. He offered her his arm, the cane in his other hand in case his leg grew weary. "Let's go practice a wedding."

Downstairs in the grand room designated for the ceremony, chairs were already arranged to create an aisle.

Lucas exchanged a glance with Jim Colby and knew the security measures they'd added were still functioning as they should. The minister had driven up from the village and claimed the roads were passable, if not exactly easy to navigate. He sounded grateful Casey had arranged for him to stay at the resort the next two nights.

Dressed in a sleek pink cocktail dress, Casey glowed with happiness. He could only imagine how much brighter she'd be tomorrow evening when the ceremony was official.

Her smile faded a fraction when Thomas wasn't there to practice pacing or his one important line. Her gaze had locked with Lucas's and he'd nodded toward her mother. He didn't want to fill in unless he absolutely had to but he would do whatever was needed of him.

As she walked down the aisle, Casey only had eyes for Levi, and Lucas knew whatever happened with her uncle, her focus was rightly on the moment of greatest importance.

Thirty minutes later the entire assembly was enjoying another festive meal. The mood was light and the guests had fun toasting the bride and groom.

Levi's mother joked about the weather and learning how

to pack a snowball, but Lucas had experienced firsthand her good aim in the earlier snowball fight.

When dessert had come and gone, Casey invited the wedding party to open the small wrapped boxes at each place setting before the guests broke apart to the various entertainments.

Levi left his seat and brought a gift to Lucas. "Mr. Camp, Casey asked me to give you this."

Lucas glanced down at the small box wrapped in the soft pink-and-mint-green wedding colors. He was surprised and a bit wary. Though he was Casey's godfather, he wasn't an official member of the wedding party. "Thank you."

Exchanging a look with his wife, Lucas carefully unwrapped the small box and opened it to find a digital key chain. Around him, others were already chatting and smiling at the images included in their similar gifts.

Lucas followed suit, but the images on his key chain weren't of today's outdoor fun, or a recollection of earlier times with Casey. He was looking at screenshots of DeRossi's personnel jacket and her itinerary for the weekend. There was even a candid shot of her with Thomas near a car at the airport.

Victoria leaned closer as he showed her. "What a thoughtful gift."

"Definitely." Across the room, he met Casey's curious gaze and saluted her resourcefulness with a quick nod. "She must have overheard me and made a call anyway."

He dropped the key chain into his pocket until he and Victoria could make a reasonable departure from the party.

Thanks to Casey's determination, maybe there was more he could do. He hoped there was something here that would prove helpful to freeing Thomas from DeRossi and the accusations she was investigating.

Chapter Eighteen

Glenstone Village, 9:38 p.m.

Jo stared out the window and up toward the snowy peak of the mountain. She could just picture the slopes dotted with skiers in a few months' time. Provided Whelan didn't blow it up in the next few hours.

The cab had been a brilliant idea and gotten them through the choke point without any problem, but now Jo had to wonder what came next. They'd spent the afternoon like a couple of tourists, walking about window shopping, holding hands and otherwise blending in.

They did make time to purchase new cell phones and clothes better suited for the weather. Even though it was a bold attempt to draw the enemy closer, nothing had happened. She hated the way their pretense made her want so badly for this to be real. Her frustration was only compounded when they'd not seen any sign of Whelan.

"We'll start again in the morning," Thomas said, coming up behind her and laying his hands gently on her shoulders. His thumbs rubbed slow circles at the base of her neck and she felt herself melting under his touch.

"It's a small town. Where else can he be?" She immediately regretted the question. "He can't be at the lodge already."

But she caught a rather predatory smile in the reflection of the window. "If he is, Lucas will handle it."

"Is that where I sent the text message earlier?"

"No. I had you send that to Jason Grant."

She spun around, shocked by his easy answer, but the truth was right there in his eyes. "Why? It's an incriminating message. One he could use to bury you."

"He's on our side." He turned her back toward the window. "He'll understand the 'wolf' is another term for Whelan. Knowing how Whelan operates and where I need to be, he'll take appropriate action. He's a genius at the tactical stuff. Used to be a sniper."

"Does he have contacts who can fly a Russian helicopter?"

"Not according to his background check."

Which she'd seen, too. She had questions, but neither of them had answers and the longer he touched her the less her brain wanted to stay engaged with the puzzle of who was behind this setup.

"But you meet all kinds of people in this business."

"Are you teasing me?" she asked.

Before he could answer, her new cell phone chimed with an incoming message. She ducked away from him to read it.

"Oh." Stunned by the message, she handed him the phone. "New intel from the office."

"What?"

She watched him read through the message detailing the new information that proved he had nothing to do with the sale or theft of the virus. "What do you think?"

"It's the same information I would have offered up in a formal defense," he said.

"I'm glad it won't go that far." They both knew formal charges would ruin his career even if he was acquitted.

"It has to be Lucas or Casey," he said, clearly stunned. "Maybe both. I'm not sure I want to know how they dug all that up considering the wedding festivities are keeping them busy."

The sadness in his voice reminded Jo how much it had hurt him to miss tonight's rehearsal dinner.

"The investigation will be officially dropped in the morning." She bounced on her toes. That was good enough news to lighten any bad mood.

His brow furrowed. "We still don't know how that virus got delivered to the cabin." He handed her the phone. "No matter what this says, no matter who changed their mind about me, Whelan isn't done. He won't back down. Not when he's this close to finishing me."

"I can live with that. For tonight." She leaped into his arms, eager to celebrate even a partial victory, and gave him a smacking kiss on the lips. "All we have to do now is get the Whelan situation under control and you'll be escorting your niece down that aisle. How does it feel, Director, to be free of the dark cloud of suspicion?"

His big hands cupped her backside. "Feels good."

"You *are* teasing me."

"I'm getting there." He rocked his hips and she felt his arousal nudging at her core.

She kissed him, lightly at first, just a soft brush of lips. But holding back wasn't an option if this might well be her last chance with him. She let the heat build, did nothing to disguise her hunger, her unquenchable need for him.

He moved toward the bed and dropped her in the deep softness of the down comforter. Laughing, she drew him down with her, wanting to touch him everywhere.

She pushed his sweater off over his head, her hands molding to the hard planes of his chest. He parted her blouse, slowly, one button at a time and she thought she'd die before his mouth finally landed hot on her breasts as he kissed and suckled the aching peaks of her nipples.

Her hands cruised over him, marveling at the strength in his sculpted shoulders, down his back. Her fingers found the old wound and she remembered avoiding this spot five years ago when it was fresh. Now it was scarred over and she wanted to feel the proof of survival.

She followed his waistband around, wedging her hands between them, eager to relearn every inch of him. He pushed her hands away and she knew a moment's panic, until she realized he only wanted to strip out of his clothing faster.

When he was gloriously naked, he tugged off her boots, dragged her jeans from her hips, and simply stared for a long, delicious moment.

"You're as gorgeous as I remember."

She didn't have the courage to ask how often he thought of those brief, passionate days. "Hurry," she said, opening to him.

His half smile told her he had no intention of following orders. He bent and pressed a kiss to her belly, working his way up to her mouth, then back down again. She was quivering under his touch, elated that her memory had served her so well. The feel of his skin against hers was almost more than she could bear. She wanted all of him…now.

When he entered her it was slow and tender and she nearly wept from the rightness of it.

Then he moved, and she shifted, wrapping her legs around him as he drove into her. The rhythm of their bodies felt as right as anything she had ever known, as right as their coming together had felt five years ago. Her climax washed over her hot and fast and she cried out, lifting her hips to meet his thrusts until he came with her and they clung to each other, both breathless and exhilarated as their bodies cooled.

When his breathing deepened and evened out, she snuggled next to his warm body, but she refused to sleep. It was her turn to keep watch. As he'd said, Whelan wasn't going to back down and she wondered how they could put an end to the threat and still make the wedding. Not much more than two hours passed before he stirred and she hadn't come up with a solution.

"You should rest, too."

"I'm fine," she said softly. Several more minutes passed and she knew he was determined to take over the watch. "What happened with you and Whelan? Why does he hate you? I understand what you cost him and how you put a smudge on his reputation but it feels like there's more."

For a moment she thought he'd shut her out as he rolled to his back and stared up at the ceiling. She drew the sheet up to ward off the chill left by the absence of his body nestled against hers.

"When I spotted him in Oberammergau I had to take action. He started with the IRA when he wasn't much more than a kid. It's a miracle he still has all ten of his fingers. He's done so many heinous things, all in the name of money and building a reputation for viciousness."

She rolled to her side and gently laid a hand on his heart, happy beyond reason when he covered it with his own. If only this could be…forever.

"The deal he was working in Germany would have cost so many lives. The Iselys were offering him the biggest payday of his career. I made a few calls, lured him away with the temptation of more cash and dumped him in Interpol hands."

He sat up suddenly and scrubbed at his face as if he could erase the memories. The scar on his back was pale and puckered against the rest of the smooth skin over solid muscle. She wished she'd done a better job with the stitches.

"I didn't know taking him out of play would mean the death of his sisters."

"What?"

He looked back at her, his eyes haunted by what he'd said, what he'd done. "Terrible, isn't it? It's the one thing I wish I could change about that mission."

"Whelan's greed got them killed, not you."

Thomas shook his head. "He would disagree."

"He's a criminal. We might make tough choices, but at the end of the day, we are all responsible for our own actions."

Thomas looked at her, amazed by the faith he saw shining in her eyes. "You're not appalled?"

"You did the right thing." She opened her arms to him. "You always do. It's one of your most admirable traits."

He went into her arms, accepting the full measure of grace she offered, and she gave for as long as he wanted.

Chapter Nineteen

Glenstone Village, 10:30 p.m.

Jason had been discussing the best course of action over lunch with the Drakes when the odd text had come through to his cell phone. Together, with dribs and drabs of intel from Lucas, the three of them formulated a plan preventing Whelan from setting a trap for the director at either choke point.

Noah guarded the road out and Jason guarded the road in to Glenstone. Blue had been assigned to watch the hotel where DeRossi had booked a room and otherwise keep an eye out for problems in the town itself.

Jason had sent Blue and Noah a message when he'd spotted the cab a few hours back, and Blue quickly confirmed DeRossi and the director arrived safely at their destination. As the day had worn on, Blue kept them updated, but by late evening they were all frustrated no one had spotted Whelan.

Hearing a car on the road, he hunkered back into his hiding place, prepared to take a shot. He was shocked when a familiar battered Jeep pulled off to the side, crunching deeper into the fresh snow.

The door opened and the dome light of the car revealed the distinctive red hair of the woman he'd spotted at the scene of the explosion. The woman Holt had warned him about. "Your presence is requested, Specialist Grant," she called out.

He didn't move.

"The wolf is sleeping."

He refused to take the bait.

"It is too cold out here for games, Grant. Mr. Camp sent me, now get in the car."

Cautiously, he made his way closer, wary it might be a trap, but only people he trusted knew his exact position. "Who are you?"

"Get in the car."

With his rifle over his shoulder, he went around to the passenger side. When both doors were closed the faint glow of the dash cast her fine features into a stark relief.

"Director Casey and Agent DeRossi are no longer suspected of any wrongdoing. I wanted to tell you myself."

"You were following them?"

"I was on assignment," she said. "Like you."

It felt like she was leaving something out very important. "That's it?"

She nodded. "You received an alert that I might be a problem."

That got his full attention. Who had that kind of access to Mission Recovery communications?

"Knowing I wanted to personally assure you I am not a problem, Mr. Camp told me where to find you."

Rather than questioning her claim, he was too busy listening to her voice. Smooth and lush. Despite the flat Midwestern tones she was using, he got the impression she could make it bend to any accent or dialect she chose. "We've met before," Jason said, instead of demanding answers he knew she wouldn't give.

"I'm flattered you think so. Now if you don't mind, I

have other business." She flicked a hand, shooing him out of the car. "Back to your perch."

"You said the wolf was sleeping."

"And it was nice of you to believe me." The Jeep groaned as she shoved the gearshift into Reverse. "But the wolf isn't my assignment. Goodbye."

Still confused, he emerged from the car, barely getting the door latched before she rumbled away. Whatever she'd said, he knew he'd seen her before.

Jason climbed back into his perch as she called it and heedless of the time difference, he sent her picture out to O'Marron for an opinion.

The lady was neck deep in this…but she was a friend of Lucas's, which was the only reason he wasn't freaking out.

Right now he had a job to do. He would figure that mystery out later.

Chapter Twenty

Thomas and Jo showed the photo of Whelan around town, finally getting another hit at a local pub at the end of High Street.

"Yeah, he was here late last night," the bartender said. "Closed the place down. And he showed back up again just a couple of hours ago. Had the French Dip sandwich with homemade chips and a beer. Was asking about renting a snowmobile." The bartender shook his head. "Claimed he was a photographer but I wasn't convinced."

Jo figured Whelan wanted to scope out the resort. She considered it a miracle he hadn't made an attempt yet. "Why didn't you believe him?"

"We get plenty of tourists and professionals through here. He and his buddy just looked like a couple idiots out to tear up the fresh snow. They'd be more likely to cause an avalanche rather than document the scenery. Besides—" he shrugged "—you ever seen a photographer on location who didn't have a camera around his neck even when he was eating?"

"Good point," Jo allowed. She caught the strain on Thomas's face. She wanted to touch him, but knew it would be more of a distraction than a comfort in his current mood.

"Did he use a credit card?"

The bartender shook his head at Thomas's question. "Not here. We're cash only."

Thomas went rigid. "We'll find him," she promised, but she knew the words were empty until the threat was contained and the wedding party was safe.

"You can't possibly rent a snowmobile without a credit card," Thomas said to Jo. He asked the bartender, "Where would he start?"

"There are a couple places to rent snowmobiles. Closest one is up one block and turn left."

"Thanks," Thomas grumbled.

The bartender leaned closer, lowering his voice. "His buddy's in the back shooting pool if you want to talk to him."

Jo grinned. Finally. They were long overdue for a break. "I'll take the friend, you find Whelan."

His dark look told her what he thought of splitting up, but they were running out of time. "Good hunting," she said.

With a resigned nod, he headed for the front door and she turned back to the bartender. "Can you point out the friend?"

"Sure." The bartender gave her the kind of smile that explained he liked helping out the ladies far more than dealing with arrogant men.

Following him to the wide archway that marked the division between dining room and pool tables, she waited, sizing up the man he said had shown up with Whelan.

She watched her target for a few minutes as he worked the table. He might pass for mid-twenties with that dark hair and youthful face, but she'd bet money he was closer to mid-thirties. Confidence shined behind an affable smile. Scanning the others in the room, she'd say his boots and jeans were too new to pass for a local. Slick, she decided, as he dropped two balls with perfect shots and botched the third.

The other spectators jeered at his miss, but she was relatively confident he'd done it on purpose, leaving his opponent with no clear play.

He was toying with his opponent, who didn't recognize the situation. Based on the thick stack of cash held down by an empty beer mug at one end of the pool table, he enjoyed the gamble.

She tamped down the urgency needling her, sensing an overly direct approach would backfire. Whether the rest of the room knew it or not, he could finish this game and walk away with the money at any point. Instead, she caught his eye and gave him a not-quite-bored smile.

His gaze slid over her from head to toe and back up again. The slow grin that followed made her want to race for the nearest shower with soap and a scrub brush.

She modified her assessment to slick with a dark side. However Whelan had connected with this guy, she'd bet he'd been more than happy to be part of the action.

His opponent at the table misjudged his bank shot and the spectators groaned in sympathy when the ball missed the pocket by the narrowest margin.

Slick stepped up to the table, his shoulders rolled back as he chalked his cue stick and evaluated the available plays. He leaned forward, prepared his shot, then sent her a wink over his shoulder.

Jo managed not to gag or roll her eyes.

He ran the table, sank the eight ball and gathered his winnings. Then he sauntered over and leaned in close. "Impressed?"

She thought he might be if she acted on the variety of ways she could take him down. "Maybe." She gave herself bonus points for self-control as she nudged him back with a finger to his chest rather than a fist to his gut. "What can you tell me about your friend Whelan?"

His grin was sharp now. "You'd like me better."

"I'm sure that's true." She flashed her identification and his eyes went wide. "Before I arrest you for accessory to murder," she improvised, "why not tell me your side of the story."

"Can we talk outside?" he said, glancing around the pool room.

"Sure." They stepped through the back door into the lane behind the pub and she was grateful Thomas and his Specialists were somewhere in the vicinity. As soon as the door closed on the music she asked his name.

"Mike Smith."

She didn't bother asking for ID. It would be fake. "How'd you and Whelan meet?"

"Look, I saw an ad online and I answered it, that's all. I didn't do anything illegal."

"What kind of ad?"

"The dude was looking for a driver who knew the area."

"And you do."

"Yeah." He shrugged. "I grew up in Denver."

Jo kept her gaze locked on Slick. There was something familiar about his face, but she couldn't place it. This guy wasn't going to be much help and he definitely didn't grow up around here. She prayed Thomas was having better luck picking up Whelan's trail. The last message from Lucas confirmed he hadn't made it to the resort yet, but it was too easy to imagine this picturesque town leveled by a crazed attempt to kill Thomas in an explosive blaze.

Even worse was the idea of the wedding party going out in the same way.

"Just tell me where he is and I'll let you off with a warning."

"He paid me to drive him around, that's all. Told me he was done and I could head back anytime."

She didn't believe him. It wasn't innocence or fear in his eyes, but calculation. Slick was stalling her and she needed to figure out why. "You stuck it out after a car exploded at the airport and even when he opened fire on another driver in Denver?"

"What? No way, that wasn't me."

She propped her hands on her hips, ready to go for her secret weapon or the nine-millimeter in the back of her waistband beneath her jacket if necessary. "Nice try but I'm not buying it. Not when we've got your handsome mug on a traffic camera leaving the scene."

"What? That's impossible."

She saw his true nature flare in his eyes, diminishing the effectiveness of the role he was trying to play. "Unless you've got a twin, we've got you cold leaving the scene of a traffic accident involving gunfire."

Slick sighed and kicked at a snowdrift. "You don't get it. I didn't have a choice."

"We all have choices." She bet the hangdog look had worked wonders on irritated mothers and girlfriends. It only raised red flags for Jo.

"He had a gun."

His words didn't fit the body language or his story. It was cold out here, but a panicked man would be sweating or fidgeting. This guy wasn't showing her any sign of nerves, only what he thought a cop would want to see. *Think!* "Forget it. You're useless to me, but stick around. The local cops will have more questions." Calculating the risk and the angles in the alley, she turned her back on him and started walking away.

She gave him points for stealth as she didn't hear so much as a footfall before he threw her to the ground. The weapon in her waistband dug into her back but she wasn't ready to go for it yet. Struggling against his stranglehold, she recognized the moves of a trained killer.

Twisting, she landed an elbow into his ear and though it was enough to startle him, the padding of her coat softened the blow too much. He recovered before she could scramble away, pinning her with a knee between her shoulder blades.

Instead of subduing her, the move only antagonized her, fueling her determination. She went limp with a small, defeated cry and when he relaxed, she flipped him, scrambling to her feet. Planting her boot into his rib cage, she pulled out the sedative disk and slapped it onto his neck. As he struggled to fight the heavy medication, she used her new cell phone to take a picture of his face.

When he passed out, she dragged him behind the Dumpster and searched his pockets. She removed his weapon and tossed it into the container. Whelan may have had a gun on him but he'd had one of his own.

"Stinking liar." She took another picture of his driver's license—Nevada not Colorado, she noticed. Taking his keys, she sent Jason a text about Slick's status. She shook her head. Men always underestimated her physical strength and ability. She straightened her hair, brushed the snow off her coat and strolled back into the pub.

Thanking the bartender, she walked out of the front door as if nothing had happened and went in search of Thomas.

He was striding down the street, the afternoon sun turning his blond hair to gold. She smiled despite the dire circumstances, because there was a picture worth having.

It was an image that would stay with her no matter how things unraveled in the next few hours.

Energized, she picked up her pace, jogging up the street to meet him.

"Did you learn anything?"

"He's not a local," she answered. Thomas's perceptive gaze was cataloging the dirt on her coat and lingered too long on her face. Precisely where her cheekbone had hit the pavement. "I'm fine," she said quickly, catching his arm when he started toward the pub. "He's incapacitated. I sent a full-face photo up the line. How about you? How much of a head start does Whelan have?"

"Too much. He already has transportation." Thomas stared up the mountain. "He could be anywhere by now. I rented a snowmobile but we might be better off with a tracker."

"Has Lucas spotted any trouble?"

"No. Not yet."

"Then we still have time."

"It's a damn big mountain, Jo."

She'd never seen him so worried or so close to defeated. She cupped his face in her gloved hands, waited until he made eye contact. "You're not responsible for Whelan's actions. We're not done until he's in custody. We know his destination."

"True, but the wedding party would be safe if—"

"Stop." She dropped her hands to his shoulders and gave him a little shake. "You know better than that. You're the director of the most elite recovery team in existence. The Specialists have a ridiculously high success rate. Think of this from the perspective of the tactical expert you are. And you'll celebrate with your friends and family when we're done."

His eyes changed, lit with the fierce, cold determination she admired. "I want this bastard, Jo."

"Then let's go get him."

He nodded and smoothed his thumb gently over her bruised cheek.

In a perfect world she'd have time to evaluate what his touch meant on a deeper level. "What's your plan?"

"We need a car. Can you call Grant?"

"No need." She pulled out Slick's keys. "We can commandeer this one." She pressed the key fob and the lights flashed on a compact SUV parked in front of the pub.

"Do I want to know?"

"Probably not."

"Okay. Stay on the main road. I'll take the snowmobile. We can flush him out, hopefully before he reaches the lodge."

He gave her a hard kiss and once more they split up.

For all the inspiration of her pep talk, she knew the challenge was as steep as the peak itself. If they weren't hours away from the ceremony, they might have asked Lucas to send out a patrol to push Whelan back toward Glenstone, but it would have to be enough that Lucas had quietly posted guards around the resort.

As she jogged to the car, she thought keeping their troubles from the bride seemed like the bigger tactical issue. She was grateful that item wasn't on her agenda.

A series of loud pops interrupted her thoughts and had her skidding along with several other people as they looked for the source of the noise. Too loud for a silenced pistol, not enough for a serious detonation. More like the sound effects from a reenactment. She drew her nine-millimeter and started for the car again, wondering if she was just paranoid enough to interrupt a show for the tourists. The next series of pops was followed by an unmistakable hissing and the faint scent of orange oil. On a curse, she hit the ground and watched all four tires on Slick's car go flat.

The whine of a snowmobile engine cut into the stunned silence on the street. Whelan. Damn it. No point racing after it. She needed a vehicle, some way to warn Thomas. On his own mad dash up the mountain, he'd never be able to answer the cell phone, even if he heard it.

Furious, tired of being jerked around, she got up and turned away from the useless vehicle. She'd find something else. No way was she leaving Thomas to deal with this monster alone. If Whelan thought to divide and conquer, to isolate Thomas on his quest for revenge, he was in for a rude awakening.

Thomas was *not* in this alone.

Jo ran back into the pub. "I'll give you $500 if you let me borrow your car until tomorrow morning."

The bartender gave her a withering look and kept drying glassware.

"Please." She pulled her wallet out of her purse and slapped several bills on the counter. "Just a few hours. I'm only going to the lodge and back. The government will pay you if anything happens to it."

After another few squeaks of towel against glass, he relented.

THOMAS LEFT GLENSTONE behind, keeping the trail map the snowmobile office had shown him in the front of his mind. It was a challenge to move slowly when he wanted to rush, but rushing never solved anything. He couldn't afford to miss a sign or clue along the way.

Thinking of how the resort was situated, he put himself in Whelan's shoes. Was the goal causing the most damage or causing Thomas the most pain? Picking his way through the trees, he crossed back and forth between the road and the ridgeline and didn't spot any sign of either Whelan or Jo. Or any other vehicles for that matter. Then again, the lodge was rented in its entirety for the wedding. No reason for anyone else to go up there this weekend.

Doubts crept in and worry like he'd never experienced threatened his self-control. No room for error on this one, personal reputation didn't matter. National security took a backseat to family security just now. His niece was counting on him to make sure this was the first day of a long and happy future.

Thomas shifted gears and resumed his hunt, the wind bringing tears to his eyes as he raced forward with renewed determination. Suddenly a tree in front of him burst into a flurry of bark as bullets bit into the trunk.

How the hell had he passed Whelan? He turned back, spotting his target on another snowmobile emblazoned with the rental company colors. Cutting the angle, he drove full throttle down the slope, cornering him as he and Jo had discussed.

But the road was empty. Where was she?

More bullets zinged by and he yanked the snowmobile behind a tree and drew his weapon to make a stand. He would not let this pyromaniac anywhere near the resort, if it was his last act of this life.

"You are out of options, Thomas, my old friend," Whelan shouted over the idling engines. "Come with me now and I will spare your family."

Thomas knew better. He risked a quick peek around the thick trunk of the tree and darted away from the machine that gave away his position. Leaving his best hope of escape was a necessary gamble. Stuck on foot now, his only option was to separate Whelan from his snowmobile. Thomas squeezed off two rounds and waited for the return fire.

"That's hardly the right answer, Director Casey."

"Who hired you?"

"Hired?" Whelan laughed, the sound full of evil intent. "I volunteered!"

Thomas ducked down as another spray of bullets rained through the trees.

"You destroyed my reputation, stole money and my family. I could not wait to return the favor."

"You forget I know your signature better than most," he called back. "You've had plenty of work since we met in Germany."

"Ah, yes, the notorious Casey network." More laughter, edging toward maniacal. "Give up! There is nothing left, Casey. The woman is dead and your family and special agency will follow."

Thomas's stomach dropped at the bleak image Whelan painted where everything that mattered most was gone. That was his intent…no matter what Thomas did right now Whelan would not stop until he was fully incapacitated or dead.

Thomas stifled the urge to leap out, gun blazing until Whelan was no more than a bad memory. If Jo was gone, and he had to believe she wasn't, the emotion had to wait. Lucas was the last line of defense for Casey and Cecelia, but Thomas wouldn't let it come to that. He had to stop this madman here and now.

On his belly, he crawled to a better position. The cold snow got up under his jacket and gloves, soaked his jeans and chilled his legs. None of it mattered.

Whelan was a genius with explosives, but if memory served, he relied on quantity over quality when it came to small arms fire. All bad guys had their weak spots.

Hearing the sound of a car engine at last and praying it was Jo, he moved to take his shot. Music blared out across the brittle air. He recognized it as an oldies station and a smile split his face. Jo loved the oldies. She wasn't dead and she'd just turned the tables once more in their favor.

Whelan opened fire on the car.

Thomas fired at Whelan but couldn't get a clear shot through the trees. True to her training, Jo reacted instinctively and Thomas wanted to cheer as she gunned the engine, forcing the car off the road, driving straight toward Whelan's position.

Countless bullets chewed up the grill, peppered the hood and punched holes in the windshield.

He said a prayer she survived the onslaught even as he took aim. Whelan reeled back as Thomas put a round through the man's shoulder.

"Damn it!"

Before he could get off another good shot, Whelan leaped onto his snowmobile and drove off toward the lodge.

Thomas leaped onto his own rental and drove to the car, immensely relieved to see Jo in one piece. "Are you hurt?"

"No. But I owe a man a car."

"Tell me later." He handed her his gun. "Let's go. When you get a shot, take it."

SHE WRAPPED HER arms around Thomas's waist and ducked her head behind his back as they raced after Whelan, staying right behind him. Leaning around Thomas, she fired at the bomber, but between the bumpy terrain and the distance, the handgun proved useless.

Thomas cut back between stands of aspen, heading for the main road, leaving the ridgeline to Whelan. If they could get ahead of him, she'd have a clear shot, but as they drove closer and closer to the lodge, she couldn't help wondering what traps Whelan, with a day's lead, had in store for them.

He throttled down and they listened to the other engine rev and struggle as Whelan urged the snowmobile up the mountain. Just before he would have shot by their hiding place, Thomas raced out of the cover of the trees, and Jo braced for the impact as Thomas bore down on him.

Startled, Whelan lost control and skidded toward the ridge, unable to leap clear as the snowmobile careened over the edge. There was a terrible explosion as the machine hit the bottom of the ravine.

Thomas pulled their snowmobile to a stop and cut the engine, but she couldn't seem to relax her grip.

"It's over." He gently pulled her hands away from his midsection. "It's done." He helped her stand and together they looked down at the wreckage. "No way he survived that," he said.

Jo thought she might be sick. A dead bomber was better than a live bomber determined to kill Thomas, but now they might never know who had assisted him in his blind rush for revenge.

Still, they had the virus and thanks to the evidence Lucas had found and submitted to her boss, the investigation was all but over. It would have to be satisfaction enough.

"You should go on to the wedding. Specialist Grant and I will clear this with the local authorities."

"No. Let Grant and Holt deal with it," he said, looking over his shoulder as a bulky, dark SUV pulled to a stop on the road. "I want you with me."

Her heart fluttered against her rib cage. The reaction was impossible to ignore even though she knew better than to read too much into the comment. It was hardly a declaration of either a personal or professional partnership.

Thomas might not want her out of his sight simply because of his longstanding trust issues. The Initiative had taken a significant stance against him and she was still the face of the oversight committee.

"There will be questions and reports," she reminded him.

"Which can all wait a few hours." Keeping her hand in his, he walked down the slope toward Specialist Grant. "You both all right?"

Jo nodded, letting Thomas explain the chase and end result. She felt Jason's gaze on their joined hands and wondered what opinion lurked behind the absolutely neutral expression on his face.

"The Mike Smith guy is already en route to our D.C. offices. The police are on the way up here," Grant said. "I'll give the statement. You two should go on up to the wedding. I'm told the roads are mostly clear, but be careful. Plows don't make regular runs up here."

"Thanks," Thomas said, opening the passenger door for her.

The heavy snowfall had turned the two-lane road into a one-lane path, complete with patches of ice where the thick stands of pine trees blocked the sunshine.

She tried to enjoy the view, reminding herself the worst was behind them. *Her.* The worst was behind her until she got back to the office. She wasn't looking forward to the fallout her full report would bring. "You know I have to mention Holt as a potential problem."

Thomas sighed, over the road or the case, she wasn't sure. "I know. He won't get any warning from me."

"Do you really suspect him?"

He didn't reply immediately and she couldn't blame him. In these past forty-eight hours, Thomas had been the victim of vicious innuendo and treacherous rumors. What he believed and what he could confirm about Holt were two different things right now.

"He's my deputy director. Your committee might have confirmed the appointment, but I'm the one who nominated him."

"Right." Her heart clutched at the distance in his voice. She noted his tight grip on the steering wheel and wondered if the road was just one challenge too many. "Do you want me to drive?"

"I've got it," he said as he eased around another shaded—and therefore icy—hairpin curve. "What do you think it would cost to extend the reservation at the resort?"

"How long?"

"Maybe forever at this rate. I could use a vacation from this long weekend."

She chuckled. "Despite the storm, it's still off-season. I'm sure they'll work with you."

"Then the front desk is my first stop after the wedding. Provided we get there in time."

Chapter Twenty-One

Glenstone Lodge

Rolling to a stop in front of the resort steps, Thomas put the car in Park and thought he might never want to drive again. Not in the mountains. Not in snow. He'd never hired a driver since taking the director's post. Maybe it was time to reconsider.

Then Jo laughed and the whole situation fell into perspective. "You made it." She tapped the clock on the dash. "You even have time to clean up."

Casey would be dressing already. Probably. Her mother would be thinking he was the worst sort of brother breaking his promise to walk Casey down the aisle. Lucas was right. He didn't know the first thing about weddings. Had his best friend been able to keep her from turning into bridezilla?

"I missed the rehearsal."

"You have one job. One short line. You'll do just fine."

His palms were damp with a sudden burst of nerves. "I don't know."

"You're nervous?" She laughed again. "Oh, this is rich. I always wondered what it would take to shatter your composure. I never would have guessed it would be a wedding."

"I'm so late. Whelan blew up her surprise. I've missed everything."

"Not the most important part." She reached across the seat, took his hand in both of hers and rubbed gently. "You're here now." Raising his hand to her lips, she kissed his knuckles. "Look, there's Lucas."

Thomas peered through the windshield. Lucas stood at the top of the steps, as calm and steady as ever. Thomas pushed the car door open and on shaking knees, climbed the stairs to join his friend.

"I—I don't know what to say." The enormity of what he was supposed to do suddenly crashed in on him.

"We'll work on it while you clean up."

"Is she furious?" Thomas didn't want her to be angry with him but she had every right. "Has she turned into a bridezilla?"

Lucas shook his head. "Resort is still standing," he said, but his smile was reserved. "She's been worried. We took turns distracting her."

"Her mother should do this." Thomas shook his head. "I don't want to screw up."

"That's how they rehearsed last night but it isn't really what Casey wants and it's her day, Thomas. She wants you." Lucas escorted him all the way to his room and when he fumbled with the key card Lucas plucked it from his fingers and swiped it, pushing the door open. "Seems a shame for you to back out now."

"You're right." He'd slogged through a frozen hell to clear his name and get here in time. "You're right," he repeated with more conviction. "There was a point when I wasn't sure I'd make it at all, much less in time to fulfill my promise to Casey."

"That's better." Lucas's smile lit up his whole face. "I'll

go let the bridal party know you're here. I'm sure the wedding planner will be happy to coach you through the steps."

"Is there somewhere for Jo to wait or dress or…" He wasn't sure he knew what he was asking.

"I believe Victoria made arrangements for her."

"Thanks, Lucas." His throat clogged with emotion. He knew this man had a hand in getting his name cleared. And the added bonus that they'd learned about Jo and made arrangements for her tugged at his heart. "For everything."

With a nod, Lucas ducked out of the room.

Thomas indulged in a shower set just shy of scalding, washing away the physical and emotional grit of the past two days.

When he emerged, he felt more like himself and ready to celebrate the wedding. He dressed, grateful for Lucas, who'd thought of all the necessities and accessories, beyond the tux delivered to the hotel, down to the cuff links that were in the luggage he'd lost to Whelan's car bomb.

Returning to the lobby, he found Lucas chatting with Levi and the other groomsmen. The wedding planner was all smiles as she directed the groom and his party to their places.

Thomas glanced over the crowd, but he didn't spot Jo. His stomach rolled at the thought that she'd left. If she had, he'd just cut the reception short and go find her. He had plans for her…for them. He was still reeling with the emotions he could no longer deny. He wanted to be with her.

"You come with me," the wedding planner said, taking his arm. "The bride will be so happy to see you."

When they reached the bride's chamber Thomas's breath caught at the sight of his niece. If it had been hard to choke out an answer when she'd asked him to walk her down the aisle, it was hopeless to try and form words now.

He opened his arms wide and she gave him an exuberant hug. Over her shoulder, he saw his sister wipe away a tear.

"Oh! Uncle Thomas," she said leaning back, fighting tears. "I was so worried."

"Sorry I'm late."

"You're just in time." She linked arms with him and her mother. "Let's get me married."

"If you're sure," he teased.

"Please. I know you vetted him ages ago."

He grinned at her. "You'll be lucky if he doesn't faint away at the first sight of you."

Casey beamed at her mother. "Should we take bets?"

Cecelia left a kiss on her daughter's cheek. "I hope Levi knows what he's in for."

"A lifetime of happiness," Casey said, sending her mother into the ceremony. Then she turned to Thomas. "It's just you and me now. And Daddy," she whispered.

Thomas touched her cheek. "He's watching, sweetie, you can count on it."

The wedding planner interrupted with a final review of his pacing, his line "her mother and I do," and where to sit after putting her hand in Levi's.

He looked down at his precious niece once more. "Let's do this thing."

Thomas got through it, though he wondered for a moment if he might pass out instead of Levi. For a man who'd spent his working life noticing details others overlooked, Thomas wouldn't have been able to describe any of the guests. He didn't see anything beyond Casey and her delighted groom.

So the warm hand that cradled his after he took his seat was a surprise, until he recognized the way Jo laced her fingers with his. He slid a glance at her and thought he owed Victoria a serious debt of gratitude.

Jo wore an amazing jade sheath that fit her petite body like a glove, and a soft, serene smile. He thought she'd never looked more beautiful and struggled to keep his eyes on the happy couple exchanging vows.

He stood with the rest of the guests, applauding as the newlyweds kissed. As the other guests moved to follow Casey and Levi from the ceremony, his sister reminded him he needed to stay for pictures.

With a gentle squeeze of his hand, Jo let him know she'd be waiting at the reception.

JO GRATEFULLY ACCEPTED a glass of white wine from the open bar. She hadn't been sure how people—primarily Lucas Camp—would receive her here. The only thing she'd decided as they'd dashed up the mountain was she wouldn't slink away into the shadows without a proper goodbye for Thomas. She'd been prepared to wait in the lobby until Thomas had fulfilled his promise to Casey, but Victoria had insisted on a different course of action.

"Thanks again for the dress," Jo said, still a little unsure how she'd fit in among this crowd.

"The shopping made me feel useful. I was getting a bit bored."

Jo wasn't sure she believed that. From what she could see, Victoria had been having a grand time celebrating another happy union with the family she'd made through the years with her Colby investigators and Lucas's Specialists.

"Lucas wasn't sure which side you were on," Victoria admitted.

Jo nearly choked on the wine, but managed a faint smile. "Most people assume I'm the enemy."

"Oversight departments have that reputation."

"And few friends. I appreciate Lucas calling off the dogs."

Victoria raised an eyebrow. "Thomas is Lucas's best friend. When he got wind of the accusations, he refused to sit back and wait."

"Your husband has good instincts." It was as far as Jo was willing to go. Maybe someday the four of them could sit down over drinks and laugh about it. Right now, it was too fresh, the averted disaster too close to destroying Thomas.

She didn't want to revisit those tense, harrowing hours; she simply wanted to revel in surviving them. "Levi and Casey make a beautiful couple and are obviously deeply in love."

"They are. It's wonderful to see love grow," Victoria said, raising her glass to encompass the rest of the wedding guests. "For years I thought my only chance had come and gone. It was no small shock to discover I could have a second chance with Lucas."

"You make a good team." Jo thought she'd never seen a couple more content and in tune with each other.

"We like to think so. It helps that we've known each other since we were very young. We were friends first. I believe that's immensely important to a relationship. Friendship and complete trust."

Jo didn't know what to say. She had the distinct impression Victoria was trying to tell her something important. It was a sweet idea, but her situation with Thomas was different from what Victoria and Lucas had found. Wasn't it? Certainly the trust part was, at least on his side.

Her heart would heal. As much as it could anyway. The past proved that much. It wouldn't be easy, but it was possible. With enough time.

"As the best friend's wife, it falls to me to say what Lucas won't," Victoria went on. "We are enormously grateful for all that you sacrificed to clear Thomas's name.

Lucas would have been devastated if anything had happened to him."

Jo felt the same, but she simply couldn't say such a thing out loud. Not without falling apart at this point. Despite her best efforts the tears brimmed and she had to look away.

Chapter Twenty-Two

Thomas was so relieved Jo had been waiting at the reception he almost couldn't sit still until the dancing began. "You did a wonderful job giving her away," Jo said as he escorted her onto the dance floor.

"I also did a full background check on him months ago."

She smiled. "But he's one of Victoria's investigators."

"Which only made it more of a challenge to get his work record."

"I think you're serious."

He didn't bother to confirm or deny.

"It was a beautiful ceremony," she said, laying her head on his shoulder.

"They're good for each other," he agreed. It was clearly a mutual devotion that went beyond the happiness and excitement of the moment. An affection that would get them through the tough times, too.

Dancing with Jo in his arms, Thomas wondered how he'd resisted her for so long. And why. If he'd been asked, he'd say Casey and Levi—two strong people—were stronger together. Until now, he just couldn't admit the same need lurked deep inside him.

How would his life and career have been different if he'd come to this conclusion years ago? Understanding the value of the present, Thomas turned his thoughts toward the here and now. And what he wanted to see tomorrow.

Both of them would have to get out of the game soon at least as far as Initiative was concerned. Just one more reason Grant had been recruited. But that was business and tonight was for family. He wanted to enjoy having Jo with him here in the moment and for all the moments they could share in the future. Years ago he'd walked away, with good reason. Her safety and his had depended on it.

He'd done good work in those years, accomplished things for the greater good and protected his country's interests. Enemies were a consequence of that, and after all his years working primarily alone, it felt different to have a partner. To have Jo.

But would she want him that way? The fiery attraction was alive and well....

"You know the minister is still here."

She glanced across the room and then up at him, her dark eyes full of laughter. "He seems to be having a grand time."

"Yes, he does." He knew he should wait, but couldn't quite remember why. They were surrounded by friends who had become family. His best friend, his brother in covert service, was across the room dancing with his own wife.

In his mind, he saw it so clearly. Lucas and Victoria could duck out with the minister and in minutes they could be married. At least in spirit. They could legalize things later.

"I never expected to feel this way," he whispered against her ear, drawing her supple body a fraction closer to his. "I won't walk away from you this time."

She looked up at him, frowned. "You didn't have a choice."

"I think I did. But I'm making a different choice now." He guided her to the edge of the dance floor and, taking her hand, led her away from the celebrating crowd. A waiter passed by and he snagged two flutes of champagne. Handing one to her, he tried to put all he was feeling into words.

"What's going on, Thomas?"

"Johara DeRossi, you've been the best partner I didn't know I needed." His throat dry, he sipped at the champagne. "These past few days you saved me, not just from an old enemy but also from myself. For the job, I armored my heart against personal attachments. Against love. Until you slipped through those defenses."

God, he wished she'd say something, but she seemed frozen, the champagne flute pressed against her lush lips.

"Marry me, Jo. Tonight. Right now."

She blinked, once, twice. "You're serious?"

It wasn't the proclamation of undying love he was hoping for. He didn't care. If someone walked away this time it wasn't going to be him. And he was leaving no words unsaid. "I love you. It's as simple as that. Whatever comes next, I don't want to face it without you beside me."

"Thomas..." Her voice quivered. "Tonight?"

His heart leaped. "If you want a big ceremony of your own we can do that, too."

She shook her head and his heart fell. A gun to his head would have been easier to face than her rejection.

"I don't need all this. I just need you." She wound her arms around his neck and kissed him. Praise God for high heels.

The spontaneous applause and catcalls surprised him into breaking the kiss long before he was ready.

"A ring might come in handy," Lucas said, joining them.

"And a couple of witnesses," Thomas replied.

Victoria caught Jo in a warm embrace. "Welcome to the family."

Thomas glanced up to see his niece in all her wedding white dragging the minister over. "He'll do it."

"Without a license it won't hold up in court, but we can go through the motions if you like," Thomas warned the woman he loved.

"We can fix that later," Jo said, smiling up at him, and Thomas felt like a new man. "Tonight's about heart and family."

Chapter Twenty-Three

Jason applauded with the rest of the guests as Director Casey and Agent DeRossi tied the knot. He was happy for the two of them, but vowed to get out of here before anyone else caught wedding-itis.

He was a confirmed bachelor and intended to keep it that way.

He spotted a flash of unmistakable red hair across the sea of wedding guests. Gin Olin. He knew her name now, thanks to O'Marron, who was convinced she was CIA. "Never a dull moment," he muttered to himself. What had brought her so close to an event populated with agents who would happily toss her down the mountainside without the benefit of a pair of skis?

He'd thought intelligence was a prerequisite for spies at her level. In the emerald-green dress with a sparkle of jewels at throat and wrist she wasn't even trying to blend in. With the Initiative investigation trashed, he had plenty of time on his hands to find out what Ms. Olin was up to.

Casey had been cleared of wrongdoing and his patriotism confirmed through official channels. The last communication Jason had received from Holt had been simply to make the most of his last few hours in Colorado. Jason was headed for Vegas for a lengthy surveillance assignment.

He watched Olin for a time, hoping to catch her talking to someone, but she merely sipped at a flute of champagne and kept an eye on him. Drink in hand, he worked his way through the crowd to intercept her and escort her off the premises. It was like dancing, he thought. Every time he advanced, she would sidestep, keeping the milling crowd between them.

Just as he decided to call in backup to corner her a waiter stepped in front of him. "Mr. Grant?"

"Yes," he replied, his gaze still locked on Olin.

"I was asked to deliver this to you."

He sent her a look. She responded with that catlike smirk.

"Thank you." Reluctantly, he turned his attention to the waiter and traded his drink for the envelope embossed with the resort logo.

The wax seal was a nice touch, he thought, sliding his finger under the flap to loosen it.

The linen notecard inside held only two words, in block script: YOU'RE NEXT.

Immediately his gaze swept the room for the sexy redhead with the killer smirk. Gone.

Tucking the card back into the envelope and the envelope into the inner pocket of his tuxedo, he reclaimed his drink and tossed it back.

As the Scotch burned its way down his throat he considered his options.

Chapter Twenty-Four

Victoria felt the small hitch in her husband's step as they waltzed at the reception. Always too proud, she knew he would dance with her all night without a single complaint if she let him.

"We really should take advantage of that cake," she said as the song came to an end. "Everyone is talking about it."

With a smile and a knowing look that told her she hadn't fooled him in the least, he tucked her arm in his and led her toward the dessert table.

They hadn't been in their seats long enough to have the first bite when Lucas touched her hand. "Did you see that?" He tipped his head slightly to a point across the room.

"Jason Grant?" She watched the man in question toss back a drink. "Trouble?"

Lucas gave her the smallest nod as he stole a bite of the delicious cake. "That's my guess."

She let the chocolate melt on her tongue, reminding herself they were retired for all intents and purposes. Ian Michaels ran the office in Chicago and Simon Ruhl took care of the one in Houston. There were plenty of smart, younger people capable of handling any concerns.

"I'm sure he'll find a way through. He's a Specialist after all."

"Hear, hear." Lucas lifted his glass. "To the best."

Victoria smiled. And that's what they were. Everyone in this room was the best.

* * * * *